D1094045

AAAAAAA-CHOOOOOOOO!!

It was one of the biggest sneezes he'd ever produced. He wiped his eyes on a blue polka dot bandana that he always carried in his left hip pocket, across from the wallet he always carried in his right hip pocket, and honked his nose. In fact, he honked it three times.

He had just stuffed the bandana back into his right hip pocket when he was seized by an uneasy feeling. Something wasn't right. The violent sneeze seemed to have changed something important in his life.

Then it struck him. The sneeze had blown his false teeth out the window! It was a dental plate he wore to replace two upper incisors, knocked out years ago when he slammed a ballpeen hammer against a pickup tire and it came back and hit him in the mouth, one of the dumbest stunts he'd ever pulled.

He was horrified that he'd blown his teeth out the window. Not only had that dental plate cost him a tub of money, but he was very self-conscious about that gap in his mouth...

He HAD to find those teeth!

the

Missing Teeth

John R. Erickson

Illustrations by Nicolette G. Earley
in the style of Gerald L. Holmes

Maverick Books, Inc.

MAVERICK BOOKS, INC.
Published by Maverick Books, Inc.
P.O. Box 549, Perryton, TX 79070
Phone: 806.435.7611
www.hankthecowdog.com

First published in the United States of America by Maverick Books, Inc. 2021.

1 3 5 7 9 10 8 6 4 2

Copyright © John R. Erickson, 2021

LIBRARY OF CONGRESS CONTROL NUMBER: 2021932782

978-1-59188-176-6 (paperback); 978-1-59188-276-3 (hardcover)

Hank the Cowdog® is a registered trademark of John R. Erickson.

Printed in the United States of America

To James William Earley, the first-born son of our illustrator, Nikki Earley, and her husband Keith. If he doesn't turn out to be a Hank fan, he'll get five Chicken Marks.

CONTENTS

CHAPTER ONE

The Mysterious Skunk Bird

It's me again, Hank the Cowdog. The mystery began in June, as I recall, yes the first week of June. Daylight comes early at that time of year and it came early that morning. The first light of the sun was already peeking through the trees and it wasn't even six o'clock yet.

At that hour of the morning, there wasn't a single dog in Texas or anywhere else who knew about the Missing Teeth. Nobody did, not even the teeth, because they hadn't gone missing at that point.

I probably shouldn't have brought up the teeth because they come later in the story and you're not supposed to know about 'em yet. Wait. They're in the title of the book so...never mind,

1

skip it. If you want to tell your mom that some teeth went missing, that's okay.

By the way, that morning sun came up in the EAST. Remember that, it might turn out to be an important clue later on. In Security Work, we never know which little facts might turn out to be important clues, so we try to remember all of them, every tiny dovetail.

Detail.

A lot of dogs hate it when the days start so early, because they have to get out of bed and go to work. They get used to the Winter Routine, don't you know, when the sun doesn't show its face until eight o'clock, and they get lazy.

That's one of the biggest problems facing America today: lazy dogs. They have no ambition or get-up-and-go. All they want to do is sleep eighteen hours a day. I have one of those mutts on my staff at the Security Division: Drover. I never saw a dog who slept so much.

I should have fired him years ago but I'm soft-hearted.

Me? I love the Summer Routine when the day starts before six o'clock and the sun doesn't go down until after nine. I'm usually wide awake at four o'clock in the morning and have to lie there for two hours until Slim drags his bones out of bed. I can't start the ranch work until he shows up, so I have to lie there, waiting. And you know me, I hate to wait.

And so it was on this particular morning of which we which. I was wide awake at four o'clock, ready to go roaring off into another day's work, but Slim and Drover were still pasted into their sheets. The only soul on the ranch who wasn't asleep, besides me of course, was a mockingbird in front of the house. The moron must have gotten his days and nights mixed up, because he was out there squawking his head off...in the dark!

They're showoffs, those mockingbirds, and think they're hot stuff because they've memorized thirteen songs they stole from other birds and seem to think that everyone on the ranch wants to hear them. We don't want to hear them. At two in the afternoon, maybe we'll be polite and listen, even though mockingbirds tend to be loud and overbearing, but when they start their noise at four in the morning...that's outrageous.

Someone needed to stuff a sock in that bird's big yap, and I was just the dog for the job. For half a minute, I gave it very serious thought, but then...I might have tumbled back into the deep hole of sleep.

Yes, I did but it wasn't entirely my fault. In

3

fact, it wasn't my fault at all and the blame must fall squarely on the stupid bird. See, it's a well-known fact that the chirping and twittering of a mockingbird can have a hypnopotomizing effect on other creatures, such as dogs. At first, it disturbs our sleep and wakes us up, then it lulls us back into slumber. It's like sleeping pills for dogs.

You know the biggest problem facing America today? It's noisy no-manners mockingbirds that spew out songs in the middle of the night and cause normally vigilant guard dogs to fall into a stuporous state. I mean, it's happening on ranches all across our land and nobody is doing anything about it.

Anyway, I was dragged back into sleep by the toxic chirps of an imbecile bird and the next thing I knew, a strange man was creeping down a dark hall and coming towards wherever I was.

Where was I? I blinked my soggy eyes and glanced around. The sun was showing its first light and I seemed to be, well, in some kind of room, perhaps in some kind of a house. What was going on? I had been awake for hours, and yet I felt as though I hadn't been awake for hours.

Then...this was creepy...the man, the strange man in the room in the house in which I was whiching, said in a gruff voice, "I'm going to

4

strangle that stinking bird!" He stomped to a device that appeared to be the front door, flung it open, stepped out on what appeared to be a porch, and yelled, "SHUT UP!"

I was in the process of doing Analysis on these events when another total stranger, this one a dog, suddenly apeppered at my side...appeared at my side, it should be, and said, "Oh my gosh, what's going on?"

I gazed into his eyeballs and saw...well, dishwater. That was my first impression, that I was looking into a pan of dirty dishwater, so I said, "You need to change your water once in a while."

To which he said, "Yeah, I need to go outside."

"Good, then you can finish the dishes."

"What dishes?"

"I don't know what dishes. You're the one who brought it up."

"No, you brought it up. All I asked was what's going on around here. I heard someone yell about a stinking bird."

I looked closer at the face. "Who are you?"

"Drover. Remember me?"

"No. Yes. I don't know. Are you the one who turned in the report about the Skunk Bird?"

"What's a Skunk Bird?"

"It's a bird that stinks. I need facts on this...

what was your name again?"

"Drover."

"Okay, let's gather up some facts on the Skunk Bird. Were you washing dishes when you saw him?"

He rolled his eyes around. "I didn't see him."

"If you didn't see him, how can you be sure he was a Skunk Bird?"

"I never said he was."

"Roy, if a bird stinks, he must be a Skunk Bird. What other kind of bird stinks?"

He uttered a groan. "My name is Drover."

"Please don't groan when I'm trying to explain an investigation."

"You called me Roy."

"Your name has nothing to do with the investigation. Now, why were you doing dishes in the middle of the night?"

"Hank, I heard someone yelling about a stinking bird and I just wondered what was going on."

"Wait a second. Are you on my staff?"

"Yeah, I'm Drover but I wasn't doing dishes."

"Okay, we'll forget the dishes. For the last time, where did you see the Skunk Bird?"

"I've never heard of a Skunk Bird."

I paced a few steps away and tried to clear my head. "Huh. Neither have I. Drover, what's going around here? What are we doing?"

His eyes popped open. "Wait a second, I just figured it out. Slim got out of bed and yelled at a noisy bird."

"You said it was a *stinking* bird."

"Yeah, Slim said he was going to strangle that stinking bird."

"Why wasn't I informed? How can I run this ranch when everyone is trying to strangle Skunk Birds in the middle of the night?"

"Hank, there's no such thing as a Skunk Bird."

My gaze flicked around the room. "Then... why are we talking about it?"

"I don't know and it worries me. Sometimes I wonder if we're normal."

That word sent a shock down my spine. "Of course we're normal, but just in case we're not, nobody needs to know. The less said about this, the better."

At that moment, the strange man came back into the house—Slim Chance. He muttered, "Six o'clock in the dadgum morning and I've got a mockingbird that wants to sing in Carnegie Hall."

Drover grinned. "Oh, I get it now. It was a mockingbird. We must have been asleep and Slim woke us up."

"You might have been asleep but I've been awake most of the night. Furthermore, I knew it was a mockingbird and, for your information, he started screeching at four o'clock. I was on this case hours ago, so don't be spreading lies."

"Then how come you called him a Skunk Bird?"

"Drover, that was your invention, not mine. You were washing dishes...were you washing dishes?"

"I've never washed a dish in my whole life."

"Then where did the dishwater come from?"

"I guess you dreamed it 'cause you were asleep. And you called me Roy too."

I stuck my nose in his face. "Listen up, soldier. I'm fixing to call you worse than Roy, and how would you like to stand with your nose in the corner for about five hours?"

"I'd rather not. It hurts my neck."

"Then let's put this whole shabby episode behind us." I marched several steps away and swept a few lingering cobwebs out of the cellar of my mind. "In these situations, it's important to remember that Life can be very confusing. Life is the problem, not us. We're just sitting in the bleachers, trying to figure things out."

"So we're not un-normal?"

"Drover, we are the very definition of normal."

"That's scary."

"What?"

"I said...oh goodie. Oh boy. I always wanted

9

to be normal."

So there you are, the start of another day at the Security Division. Drover and I had spent ten minutes in a ridiculous conversation about dish water and Skunk Birds, which don't even exist. This gives you a rare glimpse at the kinds of problems I have to deal with every day of the world. First I get no sleep, then I have to deal with a noisy bird, then I have to assure Drover that he's normal.

The terrible underlying truth is that he's NOT normal. He's not even close to normal and sometimes I'm pretty sure he's about eight bales short of a full load of hay, but I don't dare tell him the truth. It would ding his little spirit and he would bawl for a week and I would have to mop his tears off the floor.

I've said this before but I'll say it again: In many ways, this is a lousy job, I mean you figure the endless hours, the crushing responsibility, and the fact that we've got spies running all over the place. Add Drover to that mess and you've got my life.

Now...where were we? I have no idea. Things seem a little foggy.

Tell you what, let's take a break and change chapters. I'll do my Morning Exercises and we'll regroup in five minutes. Don't be late and

DON'T
    F
        A
            L
                L
                        ASLEEP!

CHAPTER TWO

Drover Ate
a Dead Fish

Z zzzzzzzzzzzzzzzzzzzzzzzzzzzzzzzzzzzzzzzzzzzzzzzz
zzzzzzzzzzzzzzzzzzzzzzzzzzzzzzzzzzzzzzzzzzzzzzzz
zzzzzzz.

    Scruff

        Muff

            Puff

                Pork

                    Piddle

                        Puddle

                            Pickle

                                Rickle

                                    Snickle

                                        Snork

                                          Murk.

    Zzzzzzzzzzzzzzzzzzzzzzzzzzzzzzzzzzzzzzzzzzzzzzz

"Hank?"

Huh? That was a man's voice. Maybe Houston was calling.

"Hank!"

I rushed to the microphone. "Houston, this is Smoke Bomb. We're circling the moon and someone is yelling, over."

"Breakfast is over and it's time to get to work."

"Houston, we must have missed breakfast and it's over, over. Send up some oatmeal and three eggs over easy, over."

"Hey! Get your carcass out of bed!"

My eyes snapped open. "Houston, we've got a humanoid creature standing over us, over. He looks mad. He's yelling and threatening our carcasses. We need the procedures on this and hurry, over."

"Hank...outside!"

Huh?

Are you with me on this? If so, tell me where we are and what's going on. At first I thought we were circling the moon in a vacuum sweeper...in a space vehicle, but that didn't check out. Number one, we didn't have a space vehicle and number two, we couldn't find the moon. Furthermore, we

13

didn't have procedures on a vacuum sweeper and we'd lost all contact with Houston.

We were in deep trouble...and maybe lost in outer space.

Wait. That humanoid creature looked familiar. I'd seen him before, maybe in a bachelor shack on a ranch. He was looking more and more like...

Huh?

Ha ha.

Okay, we need to tie up a few loose ends. Ha ha. We had a little fire in the circuits of Mission Control's instrument panel. No big deal but it caused sparks and smoke and some confusion. See, when we took that Chapter Break, I was going to run through my Exercise Program for the morning, remember? Well, something happened. I closed my eyes just for a second and the next thing I knew...

Shall we go for The Truth, The Whole Truth, and Nothing But The Truth? Here goes: Somehow my eyes slammed shut and I got dragged into a deep sleep. It happened on my watch, on my ranch, and in the middle of Slim's living room. He caught me and made a big deal about me sleeping on the job. And Drover saw the whole thing.

I offer no excuses. Well, I've got one: the mockingbird. He ruined my sleep patterns and altered my brain waves. When that happens, what's a dog supposed to do?

Even so, I'm ashamed of myself. Now the little children know a deep dark secret that I didn't want them to know: I'm vutterable to sleep.

I'm vitterable to sleep.

I'm butterable to sleep.

I'm having trouble finding the right word. I'm vinegarable to sleep.

I'm still not finding the right word and it makes me so mad, I could spit.

You know what? I don't care! If the word wants to play tricks, too bad. I have a ranch to run and I can't spend my life...

VULNERABLE. VUL-NER-A-BLE.

There we go, at last. I didn't want the little children to know it, but sometimes I'm *vulnerable to sleep* and there's no use trying to hide it.

I fell asleep. I got caught and Drover saw the whole thing. The little children know about it and I'm ashamed of myself and it will never happen again. Never.

You're probably laughing right now, because you don't believe me. You think I'll fall asleep again during business hours. Am I right about that? Go ahead and admit it and laugh all you want. But let me repeat myself repeat myself: IT

WILL NEVER HAPPEN AGAIN AGAIN. You have my Cowdog Oath on that.

Now, where were we? Oh yes, Drover's claim that he'd been up half the night, washing dishes. That was the biggest pack of lies ever told on this ranch. He has never...wait, skip the dishes. It was morning on the ranch and Slim had just awakened me up...awoken me up...he woke me up, is the point, in a rude manner.

To be honest, I couldn't blame him. I had shirked my duty and was sleeping on the job at eight o'clock in the morning. Eight o'clock! It was disgraceful but there's more to this. I saw Drover wearing an insolent grin. He loves it when I mess up and get caught.

You know, he didn't act that way until he started hanging out with Mister Never Sweat, the local cat. He used to be a nice little doggie, not too bright but a mutt with a sweet disposition, but the cat had just about ruined him. Cats will do that, I mean, they can walk past a gallon of milk and turn it sour.

Anyway, I detected his insolent grin and aimed a paw in his direction. "I saw that."

"Saw what?"

"You were grinning because I got in trouble."

"Me hee? Oh no, I'd never ha ha about hee

hee. Honest."

"Drover, grinning at the misfortunes of others is extremely rude, even cruel."

"Sorry."

"Are you really sorry or is this just another pack of lies?"

"No, I'm really hee hee."

"What?"

"I'm really sorry. Honest. Hee hee."

"Did you just laugh?"

"Oh no. It's by allergies. They're ag-ding ubb agid. By dose is stobbed ubb."

I marched over to him. "Open your mouth, I want to check this out." He opened his trap and I peered inside. Fumes rushed out and almost knocked me down. "Good grief, you smell like a dead fish!"

"Gock ock ogle ish."

"Close your mouth and try to speak a coherent sentence. Explain why you smell like a dead fish."

He closed his mouth. "'Cause I ate one."

"You ate a dead fish?"

"Yeah, Slim had sardines for breakfast and he gave me one."

"You and Slim…why wasn't I informed of this? How can I manage the affairs of this ranch when everyone is sneaking around and eating sardines?"

"Well, you were a-heehee."

"I was what?"

"You were asleep."

Now it was my turn to grin. "Soldier, you walked right into my trap. Number one, your allergies stopped bothering you when you started gloating about eating sardines."

"Oops."

"Number two, I heard you say that I was 'a-heehee.' You meant to say that I was asleep but a giggle overwhelmed you. In other words, we have irreguffable proof that you were *laughing* at the misfortunes of your commanding officer." I leaned toward him and drilled him with a steely gaze. "And on this outfit, that's a serious crime."

"Oh drat."

"And I guess you know what this means."

"Not Nose Time!"

I draped a paw over his quivering shoulder. "Buddy, your nose is fixing to get acquainted with the corner and by the time you get out, you'll be the best of friends. This court orders you to stand with your nose in the corner for..."

Slim's voice cut through the proceedings like hot butter. "Come on, you yard birds, we've got work to do. Outside!"

Drover vanished, I mean, poof.

"Drover, come back to this courtroom immediately, and that is a direct order!"

Too late. He had lit a shuck and was out the door, gone. The little sneak had managed to escape the Long Arm of Justice, but Justice not only has a long arm, it has a long memory. We had bagged his testimony and it was in our files. Sooner or later, we would slap the cuffs on him and haul him to jail where he belonged, and he would stand with his nose in the corner for hours, maybe even days or weeks.

Oh yes, Drover would PAY.

A Call From
Miss Viola

Slim was standing at the open door, waiting for me to exit the house. He wore his usual morning face (Count Dracula) and his voice had all the soothing charm of a wood rasp. "Will you hurry up?"

No, I would not hurry up. I had just suffered humiliations that no Head of Ranch Security should have to endure and I would make a slow and leisurely walk to the door. A dog has his pride and sometimes we're not in the mood to be poked and jostled around.

For the record and as a point of law, the house didn't belong to Slim anyway. It wasn't his property or his private castle. It was the hired hand's house on a ranch owned by Loper and

Sally May, which meant that it was as much mine as his. What made him think that he could order me out of my own house? The bully.

So, yes, I turned it into a walk through the park, took my time, and even stopped to scratch an itch on my left ear. Hack, hack, hack. That really put him in a twist.

"Hurry up!"

Ho hum. I gave myself a good shake and resumed my stroll. Oh...was he waiting for me? Well, darn. Maybe I could squeeze out a little more speed...or maybe not. Probably not.

But then it occurred to me...there was something about his posture, the way he was standing and holding open the screen door. It came in a flash of insight: when I slipped out the door, he was going to deliver a boot to my tail section. Of course. It was just the sort of thing he would try to do when he was in a snit.

I wiped all expression from my face, erasing all traces that I had read his mind. He didn't need to know. He was comfortable, living with the delusion that I was just a dumb dog who slept all the time. Ha. Let him think whatever he wanted.

He had no idea what goes on in the mind of a dog.

I continued my slow stroll. I could see embers of

fury glowing in his eyes and a weird twitch on his lips. This guy was boiling inside and...yes, I saw him cock his right leg, like the hammer on a pistol.

This would have to be quick and precise, a well-timed Sprint Maneuver. One little error in the calculations would blow the op.

Eight inches in front of the open door, I reached up to the Console of My Mind and pressed the Launch Button, igniting engines one and two in a sudden burst of flames. I flew through the opening! He aimed his boot at a hiney that wasn't there and got nothing but thin air.

On the other side, out on the porch, I rolled my eyes around and gave him a casual look. I didn't want to rub it in, but...*yes, I did want to rub it in!* Why not? I gave him the snottiest look I could devise, a look that said, "Gosh, you missed."

It ripped him, oh, it ripped him! He sputtered, "Knot-head. Dumb luck beats brains every time."

Well, he could call it whatever he wanted, but I had won a huge moral victory and he could spend the rest of the day pouting about it. I really didn't care.

Hee hee. I loved it.

We started walking toward the pickup. It was time to knock off the foolishness and get back to work. I had a long list of jobs on the ranch that needed to be...

Remember that mockingbird, the one who'd been screeching his playlist of stolen bird songs at four o'clock in the morning? Well, he was still at it, now perched on the cross-arm of a utility pole beside the saddle shed, belting out the same old tiresome tunes we'd been listening to for the past five hours: "Bobwhite Quail," "Rain Crow," "Cardinal," "Mourning Dove," "South African Tweet-Tweet," and others I couldn't identify.

I was sick of that guy and his noise, so I swung my guns around and gave him several blasts of barking. It did no good, of course. Mockingbirds are like cats, they don't take hints. But Slim chunked a rock at him. He missed the bird but hit the pole and I guess the dummy got the message: When your audience starts throwing rocks, it means *they don't like your music!*

He flew away to torment someone else and that brought a smile to Slim's pouting mouth. "Serves him right. Stinking bird."

Stinking bird?

Data Control kicked in and launched a search of our case files. Hadn't we worked a case that involved a stinking bird? Yes, I was sure we had and it involved the elusive Skunk Bird. All at once the clues were...

Wait. Skip that. It was a bogus report, probably planted into our systems by the cat. Never mind.

Just as we reached the pickup, the soft morning air was fractured by a strange ringing sound. My ears shot up and I glanced at Slim. He'd heard it too. It wasn't the mockingbird.

He rolled his eyes and growled, "it's the dadgum phone, probably Loper. What does he want?" He started walking back to the house and, well, I followed, of course. That's what we do. The phone continued to ring and he continued to growl. "I'm coming! Ring all you want, I ain't going to speed up, 'cause I don't take orders from a telephone."

Those were brave words, him saying that he didn't take orders from a phone, but it kept ringing and, in spite of himself, he picked up the pace. He walked faster, then actually broke into a jog-trot, which was totally out of character. I mean, Slim Chance was *not* a jogger or a trotter, especially in the morning.

This next part is kind of hard to explain. As I've said before, those of us in the Security Division are trained to follow the lead of our people. When they walk south, we walk south. When they walk north, we walk north. When they kick up the pace and start jogging, we're right there, jogging beside them.

But somehow...well, one of us got out of his lane, you might say, and Slim's long skinny legs got tangled up with the various parts of my amazing body. He took a little spill as we were hoofing it up the porch steps, is the point, and it threw us a little behind. By the time he made it inside the house and snatched up the phone, nobody was there.

Uh oh. His eyes bulged, his face turned red, and his mouth became as thin and gray as a stub of welding rod. I braced myself for something really crazy—him jerking the phone off the wall and flushing it down the pot, or something like that. I mean, I've known the guy for a long time and have seen him do some crazy things.

The air inside the house fell deathly still. I could hear our breathing, his and mine. His eyeballs flicked back and forth, and my tail kicked into Automatic Wags of Concern—the equivalent of someone on a battlefield, waving a White Flag of Peace. Hey, I didn't want this deal to get out of hand.

It worked. Instead of going off like a keg of powder, he dialed a number and placed the receiver against his ear...the left ear, as I recall. It rang several times—the phone, not the ear— then: "Loper? Did you just call me? Good."

That was it. He hung up the phone and stood there for a long time, chewing on the soft tissue of his left cheek. (Left ear, left cheek. I made a note of that, I mean, you never know).

At last he spoke. "If it wasn't Loper, who could it be? Nobody ever calls me. I've paid my bills and didn't write any hot checks. Must have been a wrong number. Good. There ain't one person in this whole world I want to talk to."

He walked toward the door and, well, of course I followed. Then I heard him say, "Viola." He stopped all of a sudden and I ran into his legs. He twisted around and hissed, "Will you quit follering me around? You're worse than a guilty conscience."

Well, excuse me! What did he want, some mutt who didn't give a rip about his job, who sat on the porch and snapped at gnats? You know the biggest problem facing America today? *People who won't let the dogs do the work they were designed to do!*

No wonder things are in such a mess.

Oh well. He went back to the phone and dialed a number. This time, he held the receiver to his *right* ear. (I made a note of that). "Hello? Viola? By any chance, did you try to call me just now? Oh. Sorry, I was outside." He listened for a while and his face grew solemn. "I see. Okay,

I'm on my way." He hung up the phone and mumbled, "They can't find Woodrow."

Hmmm. That didn't sound good.

He headed for the door and, whether he liked it or not, I fell in step right behind him. I've said this before but I'll say it again: We follow our people through good times and bad, into battle, into fire and into blizzards. That's what we do. Whether or not they deserve it is another question, and most of the time, THEY DON'T.

You know the biggest problem facing America today? We've already covered that, so never mind.

The point is that I followed Slim out of the house, across the porch, down the steps, and to his pickup. If my presence reminded him of a guilty conscience, I didn't care.

Along the way, guess who showed up: Little Mister Bail-Jumper, Mister Half-Stepper. He flashed a silly grin. "Oh, hi. Where are we going?"

"Don't speak to me, you little wretch."

"Gosh, what did I do?"

"What did you do? Ha. The list is so long, we'd need a truck to haul it."

"I've always wanted to bark at a truck."

"What?"

"I've never had the nerve to bark at a truck. Have you?"

I couldn't believe this. "Of course I've barked at trucks."

"Yeah, but I mean the big ones. They're huge and loud, and they've got all those tires."

I studied the perplexed look on his face. Did I have time to school this ninny? After he had sprinted out of the courtroom and jumped bail? I mean, those were serious offenses on my ranch. What he really needed was a thrashing, not an education. At the very least, he needed to be shunned and ignored for a month or two.

The Tennis Ball of Life whizzed back and forth across the Net of...Something: yes, no, yes, no. Would I help him or not?

It was a toughie, but you know me. I'm hard-boiled on the outside because, well, in this business, we have to be tough. If I turned into a powder puff, the crooks and the cat would take the place over and run it straight into the ground, and we're talking about pure chaos and corruption.

But penetrate the outer layers of steel and iron and steel and you find a dog who understands that...well, genius must be shared. That's another part of my job, and very impointant. If there's a noodle-brain out there who needs to be lifted out of the depths of ignorance, we need to pause and help him.

And there *was* such a noodle-brain, right there beside me.

Okay, I would try to help him.

This next part is very emotional. It might bring tears to your eyes, so you'll need tissues.

Woodrow Is Missing

Okay, there we were, the noodle-brain and I. I seized a sneeze...I seized a big gulp of air, that is, and began my lecture on Trucknology.

"Drover, every big job consists of several small jobs. With those big trucks, you take 'em one axle at a time. The big 'uns have five axles, two on the trailer and three on the truck. I start at the left rear and work my way to the front."

"I'm afraid my rear would get left right away."

A deep silence loomed between us. "Are you trying to be funny?"

"Well, I thought it was kind of cute, 'my rear would get left right away.' Hee hee."

"Please don't try to be cute in the middle of my lecture."

"I don't think it was the middle. You just started."

"Hush. Don't try to be cute or funny at any point in my lecture. Now, where was I?"

"You left your rear right on the axis and started toward the frump."

"That is exactly wrong and I hope you'll pay attention. I said...I start at the left rear *axle* and work my way to the *front*."

"Oh yeah, maybe that was it."

"And I must emphasize that speed is crucial. Slow pokes don't make the cut."

"You cut the tires?"

"Negative. We seldom do a hard bite on the tire, maybe just a few nips. Put a hard bite on a moving tire and it will thrash the snot out of you."

"Boy, this is interesting. How many barks on each tire?"

"Good question. A lot of mutts blast away on the first axle and blow all their energy. They've got nothing left for the rest of the job. One axle and they're out of the game."

"I'll be derned, I never would have thought of that."

"Yes, well, this is science, Drover, not rocket surgery. Speed is important on a Truck Job, but not everything. No dog shuts down a truck with speed alone. It comes down to endurance. The

big boys have five axles and eighteen tires, and you have to blast every one of them with Secret Encoding Fluid."

He was shocked "All eighteen?"

"Yes sir, every last one of 'em. That's the part most mutts don't know about."

He gasped. "Oh my gosh, I'd never be able to do that. You've actually done it?"

I had to chuckle. "Not once but many times."

"Didn't you get dewaterfied?"

"You mean dehydrated? Only once. It was a hot day."

He almost swooned. "No wonder you're Head of Ranch Security!"

This caused me to blush a little bit. "Well, what can I say?"

By that time we had reached the pickup. Slim was there, tapping his toe and holding the door open. In his usual charming manner, he growled, "Get in."

He had no appreciation for the demands of the Teaching Profession. None.

I leaped into the cab and took my usual Shotgun Position. Drover tried to leap up into the seat and, as usual, fell back on the ground. Slim had to pitch him inside.

As we pulled away from the house, I experienced a kind of tingle or glow...of pride, I suppose.

There are many unpleasant parts to this job, but the Teaching Aspect brings a lot of satisfaction. Drover would never succeed in doing a Truck Job, I knew that, but at least he had some idea of how much he didn't know about Trucknology.

When we can lift a dunce a few inches out of Dunceville, it kind of makes our day.

We left Slim's place and motored down the county road to the house where Viola lived with her aging parents. I found myself stealing glances at Drover. He wasn't whining about having to sit in the middle, away from the window and its pleasant breeze, and that was unusual. Furthermore, he was wearing a little grin that seemed...what is the word? Smug? Self-satisfied?

It made me curious. "What are you grinning about?"

"Who me? Was I grinning?"

"Yes. That's why I asked. Why are you grinning?"

"Oh, I don't know. Maybe it takes less effort to grin than to frown."

"Hmm. Maybe so." Another minute passed. "Wasn't I mad at you about something?"

"Well, let me think here." He wadded up the left side of his face and threw a ripple into his lipple...into his lip. "Nope, I don't think so. You haven't gotten mad at me in days."

"Really? I could have sworn…"

Hm. I could have sworn that I'd gotten mad at him about something, and not so long ago. Oh well. If you can't remember why you were mad, maybe you weren't mad enough to remember and you should just forget it…because you already did.

Heh. I like that one. Did you get it? "If you can't remember why you were mad…" Maybe you got it.

Where were we? Oh yes, Trucknology. It's kind of hard to believe, but eighty-seven percent of all the dogs living in America today don't know beans about barking trucks. They'll yap at a bicycle or a scooter and think they're hot stuff, but put 'em up against a big eighteen-wheeler…I think we've already covered that.

We were driving down the county road, is the point, on our way to see Miss Viola, and just the thought of her caused flutterations in my heart. Yes, I understood that she was engaged to Slim Chance and wore his ring with the microscopic diamond, but she and I had always enjoyed a special kind of relationship.

She was crazy about me.

Maybe you have to be a dog to understand it… or maybe even dogs can't grasp it. But hey, if it's real and true, it doesn't have to be understood.

It's just there. And the thought of seeing her again made my heart go "pitty-pat."

She lived with her folks in a big old two-story house, down the creek from Slim's place. It was only three miles away but Slim drove like a snail so it took us ten minutes to get there. He drove like a snail because he was checking every little detail of everything we passed: cattle, wild flowers, fences, the grass, and the sky.

He seemed particularly interested in the morning sky. "Those clouds have a stormy look."

He switched on the radio, the same one whose antenna was a wire coat hanger. Years ago, a bale of hay had slid off the load and sheared off the factory antenna, and since the coat hanger had worked pretty well, nobody on the ranch had bothered to buy a new one.

Anyway, Slim switched on the radio and got the weather report: a Severe Thunderstorm Watch for the Oklahoma and Texas Panhandles. Then came the morning news about politics, explosions, scandals, and corruption in high places.

That didn't last long. Slim snapped it off and said—he appeared to be speaking to the radio— "You ain't going to ruin my day. I've got dogs who can handle that."

What was that supposed to mean?

When we pulled up in front of the house, Viola and her mother were out on the porch. Her mother, Rosella, sat in the glider swing, her hands folded in her lap, and Viola was pacing and looking at the clouds.

Slim got out and gave us a hard glare. "Y'all stay in the pickup."

Aye aye, sir.

I waited a full minute before I bailed out the window and raced past him. I heard him mutter my name, but what did he expect? I hadn't seen Viola in a whole week and knew she was aching to see me. She was but, well, she had worry written all over her face. She gave me a quick smile and a pat on the head and went straight to Slim. Rats.

She filled him in on the morning's events. I listened carefully and took detailed notes. You want to see them? I guess we have time.

Detailed Notes

1. Woodrow got up at his usual time, 5:00 a.m., and went through his normal morning routine. He made coffee, ate two pieces of buttered toast with wild plum jelly, and read *Livestock Weekly* until the sun came up around 5:45.
2. He got into his pickup and drove out into the

pasture to look at the cattle and check to see how many sprigs of grass had grown overnight.

3. The ladies got up around seven and fixed breakfast. At seven-thirty, Woodrow hadn't returned. That was unusual.

4. At eight o'clock, Viola went looking for him. She checked the shop, the barn, and the heifer pasture and didn't find him.

5. At eight-thirty, she was worried that something had happened to him and called Slim.

End of Report

Please Put In Shredder With 1 Head of Cabbage and 2 Onions

Slim listened and nibbled at his lip. "Well, that don't sound like Woodrow."

"No, he always follows the same routine. I'm worried."

"Any chance he went to town?"

"Oh no. He's even more of a hermit than you."

"Would he be visiting one of the neighbors?"

She rolled her eyes. "Not likely. The last I heard, he was mad at all them."

"That sounds like him. So he's somewhere on the ranch?"

"That would be my guess. Maybe his pickup quit on him or he had a flat."

"Most likely, that's it. Well, I ain't exactly Daniel Boone, but maybe I can find some fresh tire tracks." He pointed to the sky, where a big line of whitish clouds was creeping in from the north. "That's liable to be a problem. I need to find him before the rain hits."

"Should I go with you? I could open gates."

Slim studied on that. "No, you stay with your mom. By any chance, do y'all have some walkie-talkies?"

"Yes, Daddy keeps them in his shop and he makes sure the batteries are always fresh."

"That's a weird way of doing things. On our outfit, Loper makes sure the batteries are always dead."

Five minutes later, Slim had one of the walkie-talkies clipped to his belt and we were ready to roll. He put his arm around Viola. "Try not to worry. He's probably fine. I'll let you know."

Drover didn't show up for Pickup Loaderation and as we drove south in the pickup, I saw him lying on the porch, staring with moon eyes at Miss Viola. The runt actually thought she liked him. He could be so childish!

I made a mental note to add five Chicken Marks to his record.

We Find
Woodrow's Pickup

We crossed a cattle guard, entered the heifer trap, and followed a pasture road for a while, until we came to a sandy spot in the trail. Slim got out and studied some tire tracks in the sand. "Those tracks are fresh. He went this way."

We kept driving south, then east, crossed another cattle guard, and entered a big flat meadow on the south side of the creek. This was Woodrow's hay meadow, where he baled up prairie hay every summer.

Slim's eyes were prowling the country ahead and I was...to be honest, my attention had strayed. Somewhere along the line, I had picked up a sandbur and it had lodged between two toes on my right front paw. I had tried to ignore it but now it was starting to get on my nerves.

A sticker between your toes doesn't sound like a big deal, but it is. It won't shut a dog down entirely but it's like driving a pickup with a flat tire. It'll cause a limp, is the bottom line, and I needed to fix it before we got any deeper in the investigation.

We have a special procedure for sand burs and it's not simple. A dog has to click his teeth together in a rapid motion to seize and remove the bur, which I did. The next problem was that the sticker stuck to the end of my tongue.

Have you ever had a sandbur embedded in your tongue? It almost caused a runaway, I mean we're talking about shooting out my tongue as far as it would go and slapping it with my paws. That worked, finally, but then the cursed thing was stuck to the bottom of my paw.

It wasn't funny but guess who was watching it with a big grin: my friend and cowboy companion, Slim Chance. He thought it was hilarious and said, "Hank, you've got more ways of looking ridiculous than any dog I ever met."

More ways of...I couldn't believe he said that! For his information...

He stopped the pickup. "You're a disobedient hound and don't deserve any help, but hold still and I'll pull it out."

No thanks, I could handle my own...okay, maybe just once.

I surrendered my paw. He made tweezers with his thumb and finger, pinched the sticker, and removed if from my paw. Then it got funny. The sticker dug into his right thumb. "Ow!" He used his other thumb and finger to pull it out and it stuck into his left thumb. He muttered and grumbled, tried to shake the sticker off his thumb (didn't work), and finally flicked it out the window with his right index finger.

He studied his thumb, which had sprouted a little dot of blood. "We spend half our lives trying to keep a sharp edge on drill bits and knives. Stickers never sharpen anything and they never get dull. That really burns me up."

I beamed him a look that said, "Slim, you've got more ways of looking ridiculous than any man I ever met. Hee hee." I wish I could have said it out loud.

He started the pickup, put 'er in gear, and we resumed our mission to...I had already forgotten what we were doing out there in the hay meadow which, by the way, was still boggy from spring rains. Hay meadows are always boggy in a wet spring because they're located in areas where water is close to the surface, don't you know. When rain water falls on top of ground that's already wet, you get "slews," shallow swampy pools of water.

In the heat of summer, those slews dry up and the hay crew comes in with mowers, hay rakes, and balers and bale up the tall grass, but now it was pretty swampy. Lucky for us, the road was built up higher than the rest of the field, else we might have buried the pickup in mud.

You don't drive across a hay meadow in the spring. That's a serious no-no.

Hmm. Come to think of it...remember that line of whitish clouds that was creeping in from the north? Well, they were now directly overhead and looking rather...you know, a guy might not want to be driving around a boggy hay meadow during a rain storm. Maybe...

At that very moment, I heard Slim say, "There's the pickup."

Huh?

What pickup? Oh yes, the pickup. We'd been searching for Woodrow's pickup, and sure enough, I saw it in the distance, sitting near a grove of cottonwood trees. Slim kicked up the speed and drove to it. He stopped and we got out.

I raced to the vehicle and slapped a mark on the

left rear wheel, proof that Slim and I were the first responders who responded first. Then I marched around the pickup and began amassing clues.

Slim looked inside the cab. "He ain't here."

Yes, I could have told him that. I had already checked.

He pulled the...what had he called that thing on his belt? The "wicker-walkie?" "Ticker-talkie?" He pulled the ticker-wicker from his belt and put it to his mouth. "Viola, can you read me?"

This was pretty weird. All at once I heard Viola's voice. She said, "I hear you, go ahead."

"I found his pickup in the hay meadow. He didn't get stuck. Looks like he got out and took off walking." A big fat raindrop splattered on the end of his nose. "And I think it's fixing to rain. Call the sheriff's office and tell Deputy Kile to head this way. We may have to mount a search for your daddy."

"Oh dear."

"I'll start looking...if I can."

"All right, thanks. Be careful."

Slim clipped the thing back on his belt. You know what? Unless I was badly mistaken, Slim and Viola had somehow *talked to each other* over the ticker-wickers! Amazing. You know, the Security Division could have made good use of that kind of equipment, but it would never happen. The dogs are at the bottom of everyone's list for new equipment.

Oh well, it was time to launch an S&R for Woodrow. (That's our shorthand term for Search and Rescue, don't you know). First thing, I trotted a circle around the pickup, sniffing the ground. We call it "cutting for sign." The idea is to pick up the scent and tracks of anyone who walked away from the pickup. Here, let's draw it out on the blackboard.

Okay, first off, we'll write down the word "PICKUP" and draw a circle around it. You see that chalk circle? Well, anyone leaving the vehicle has to cross the circle and when he does, he leaves some kind of sign. What the investigator does is...

You know, this seems kind of obvious, so let's skip it. The point is that I was on the case and right away I found tracks. At first they resembled coon tracks but we're trained never to fall for the obvious, so I switched on Nosetory Sensors and began...

"Hey, birdbrain, his tracks are over here."

Huh? Okay, that was Slim's voice and...I knew they were coon tracks but we have to check out every lead. I rushed over to the spot where Slim was pointing to fresh boot tracks in the ground.

"Them's the tracks we're trying to follow."

Yes, of course, I knew that. They were human boot prints, obviously left by a human wearing boots. I scanned the tracks with Snifforadar and memorized the profile. Mud. They smelled exactly like swamp mud...and so did everything else. Not very helpful.

Even so, I put my nose to the groundstone and led the way. I'll let you in on a little secret. I get a thrill out of taking Positions of Leadership. Some dogs are meant to lead and some dogs, most of them, are meant to follow along behind and say "duh."

Me? I was born to lead and, yes, I would be taking the Primary Scout Position on this mission, a very important...

"Hank, the trail's over here."

On the other hand, it might be better to let Slim take the lead position. He was taller, don't you see, and had a better overall view of the so-forth. In these deals, we can't be selfish. We have to work as a team.

So, yes, I sent Slim ahead in the Primary Scout Position, while I took the equally-important Secondary Primary Scout Position, right behind him. It was equally important because I had to monitor the rear to be sure we weren't being followed.

Who would be following us across a marshy hay meadow? Well, we never know and that's why we have to keep a close watch, and that's why we always put our sharpest personnel in the Secondary Primary Scout Position. We don't want to get ambushed.

Anyway, we had gone, oh, twenty yards toward that grove of cottonwood trees when a spear of lightning sliced through the sky, followed by a bone-rattling blast of thunder. When my ears recovered from that, they began picking up... what was that roaring sound? It was a steady roaring sound that seemed to be getting louder... and closer. I wondered...

RAIN!

Buckets of rain. Firehose. Waterfall. And a hard, cold wind.

We were blind! We were drowning! Even so, I led our unit back to...

"Hank, the pickup's over here!"

We staggered back to the pickup, is the point. Slim pried open the door and we fell inside, soaked, dripping water, and gasping for air. Slim's hat was limp and his hair looked...well, awful, what else can you say? Water streamed down his cheeks and dripped off his chin and he had to wipe the lenses of his glasses on his shirt tail.

I wasn't much better. Drenched. But we dogs have procedures for coping with drenchness. We

shake. I closed my eyes, straightened my tail, and created an earthquake that went through my entire...

"DON'T SHAKE INSIDE MY PICKUP, YOU DONKEY!"

Huh?

He'd seen a donkey? I opened my eyes and shot a glance around the cab. I saw no donkeys, only...yipes, Slim was wearing a dangerous expression, I mean, pinched eyes and curled lip and flared nostrils. What was going on here?

"You sprayed frazzling water all over my pickup."

Oh. Well, I was drying myself off. Those things happen.

"And you know what else? You stink." He leaned toward me. "Pooch, nobody loves a wet dog."

Really? I could hardly believe that.

He started cranking down the window to get some fresh air, I suppose, and got a face-full of cold rain, I mean, it was raining snakes and weasels out there. And pitchforks. He rolled up the window and shook his head...as water dripped off his nose and ears.

"This ain't going to be fun, I can already tell."

CHAPTER SIX

A Hooded Executioner!

Ho hum. Boy, time sure did crawl.

Slim and I were trapped inside a pickup in which neither of us wanted to be trapped in which. Rain was pouring down and it roared on the roof of the pickup. The windshield had become a gray blur, so we couldn't see anything outside. The air in the cab was cold and damp and smelled like a cellar full of wet cats. Slim was mad at me and worried about Woodrow.

Yes, time sure did crawl. After what seemed a month, he decided to turn on the radio and listen to some music. He switched it on and got a loud buzz. He shook his head and mumbled something, then noticed the problem: the wind had blown the coat hanger antenna off its stub.

He drummed his fingers on the steering wheel. "I guess we could tell jokes. You know why the Little Moron took a pair of scissors outside on a dark night?"

Uh…no.

"He wanted to see an ee-clips." He stared at me. "Get it? Scissors, clips, eclipse."

Okay. Ha ha. Great joke.

"You want to hear another one?"

No.

"How come the Little Moron jumped off the Umpire State Building? 'Cause he wanted to make a big splash on Broadway." Silence. "You're supposed to laugh, dog. It's a joke. It's funny and you've got nothing better to do."

Ha ha. This was embarrassing.

Of course he wasn't satisfied and went spinning off into more nonsense. "I'll bet Mark Twain told jokes to his dog and I'll bet the dog was smart enough to appreciate great humor. You wouldn't know a joke from a bowl of poke salad."

Sometimes I have to ignore him.

At last he quit grumbling and we fell into silence…which wasn't very silent, with the constant roar of rain on the roof. I mean, this was serious rain and it went on and on and on. I thought I might die of boredom, but then he sat up straight and grinned.

"Wait. I just thought of a great song about rain in the Panhandle, but I ain't going to sing it for you 'cause you've got no class or taste...unless you was to beg and then I might."

Sigh. All right. Beg beg beg beg beggity beg.

"Well...okay, if you really, really want to hear it."

I *didn't* really, really want to hear it, but he didn't care. He sang it anyway, right there in the pickup, in front of an audience of ME.

The Great American Desert

The Great American Desert is what they
   called this place.
Flat as a table, it stretched out before them
   through endless time and space.
There wasn't a tree or even a shrub to
   break the horizon's brink.
It looked like an ocean but there was a catch:
   you couldn't find water to drink.

And that's why they called it a desert,
It didn't have faucets or sinks.
It looked like an ocean without H2O
And it didn't have water to drink.

This Panhandle country is famous for all
   kinds of weather events.
Our wind is so windy, it'll straighten the
   chain you left tied on a fence.
Our blizzards are famous and so are the
   droughts that inspired many a tale.
The annual rainfall in this arid land ain't
   enough to put rust on a nail.

   And that's why they called it a desert,
   It didn't have faucets or sinks.
   It looked like an ocean without H2O
   And it didn't have water to drink.

I'm thinking of that this morning in June,
   inside the cab of my truck.
I'm breathing stale air that smells like wet
   dog in weather that was made for a duck.
Maybe my eyes have deceived me but I
   think that I'm watching a flood.
It looks like an ocean 'cause that's what it
   is, with lots of fresh water and mud.

   Right now, it ain't the Sahara.
   This country can change in a blink.
   Just roll down the winn-der and open
      your mouth,

There's plenty of water to drink. Today.

A guy could even go swimming
And a short-legged man might drown.

He finished the song and heaved a sigh of contentment. "Hank, I'll tell you in strictest confidence, my music agent is crazy about that tune." He glanced around and whispered behind his hand. "He wants to fly me out to Nashville and put me on a bunch of talk shows. He thinks we could be Number One on the charts by the Fourth of July. I'll be driving around town in a limo that's longer than a football field." He winked and grinned. "But don't tell anyone. Shhh. Right now, it's just between us dogs."

Oh brother. What can you say? Do other people behave this way around their dogs?

We lapsed into another long silence and Slim's face lost its luster of fame. "Man alive, I hope Woodrow found some kind of shelter. This is awful!"

At that very moment...you won't believe this, hang on to something...at that very moment, we heard a mysterious tap on Slim's window and through the foggy glass, we saw...A MAN'S FACE, and he was wearing some kind of creepy hood!

Well, you know me. When I see a face where

there shouldn't be a face and a man in a hood in a place where a man in a hood shouldn't be, the hair on my back stands up like a wire brush and, fellers, I BARK! I pumped out three big ones all in a row, back-to-back.

Slim seemed as shocked as I was. For a long moment, he froze and stared, then muttered, "Bobby? Good honk!"

Bobby? Was this some kind of hooded executioner named "Bobby," someone Slim knew?

That didn't make any sense. Hooded executioners don't have common names like Bobby and Slim didn't know anyone who wore a dark hooded robe, so I kept pumping out the barks.

"Hank, dry up. It's Deputy Kile."

Deputy Kile? That was impossible! How...

A moment later, the door on my side flew open and a man dived inside, dripping water from a... huh? Okay, ha ha, it was a rain poncho, not exactly a hooded robe, but it sure looked like the black hooded robe of some creepy guy who went around carrying an axe and chopping off the heads of people and dogs.

Don't laugh. What would you have thought if you'd been there? I mean, we were out in the middle of nowhere.

Slim gave him a nod. "Welcome to the Great American Desert. You reckon it's going to rain?"

"Last night, they said we had a 50% chance. I think we've gotten every bit of that."

"Let me guess. You came down here in a squad car without four-wheel drive. Now you're stuck and need me to bail you out."

Deputy Kile mopped his face with a bandana. "Something like that."

"Bobby, when Viola called the sheriff's department, she didn't know they'd send down some rookie detective who wasn't equipped for the weather."

"Nobody said that we'd get three and a half inches of rain or that Woodrow's hay meadow would turn into a swamp. Any sign of him?"

"I found some boot tracks and was trying to follow 'em toward that grove of cottonwoods, then the rain hit."

"I don't suppose you tried yelling his name."

Slim was silent. "No, didn't think of that."

"Rookie mistake. Those tracks'll be gone now and we've got nothing."

"So what's your plan?"

"My plan was pretty simple, to find you and then search for an elderly gentlemen who's gone missing. My plan is trash."

Slim tried to look out the window but it had fogged over. He wiped it with the back of his hand and he still couldn't see much. "We can't look for him till the rain quits, so we might as well pull your car out of the mud. It'll save us time on the other end."

The deputy scrunched down in the seat and rested his knee on the dash. "Slim, in my line of work, we always consider the possibility that Plan B might be worse than Plan A, so we look at a third option. Plan C means 'sit tight and do nothing.'"

"Bobby, I've been cooped up in this pickup for an hour, telling jokes to a dog. I'm fixing to go nuts."

"What if you get the pickup stuck trying to pull me out?"

"This rig has four-wheel drive and good radial tires. It's never been stuck, and Loper and I have plowed mud on wheat pasture that you wouldn't believe."

"You got a nylon tow rope?"

Slim swallowed. "No."

The deputy sighed. "What kind of guntsel outfit is this?"

"Bobby, when I left the house, it's wasn't pouring rain."

"When you go to work in the spring, you carry a tow rope. Roy Rogers and Gene Autry always carried a tow rope."

"Roy and Gene were horseback most of the time."

"Roy had a Jeep."

"Never mind Roy. Did you bring a tow rope?"

The deputy grinned. "Of course I did. It's standard equipment for people who know what they're doing."

"Should we use it or sit here talking about Roy and Gene?"

The deputy fanned the air in front of his face. "When was the last time you gave that dog a bath...with soap?"

"It's been a while. You want to try it or not?"

"I'm a believer in Plan C, but I guess you're going to do something, even if it's wrong."

"Good call." Slim started the motor. "You're lucky you've got me to bail you out of your messes."

He put the pickup in four-wheel drive and off we went on a new adventure. It turned out to be pretty adventurous, so you'd better keep reading.

CHAPTER SEVEN

A Muddy
Adventure

The pasture road was pretty greasy but Slim had the pickup in four-wheel drive and we plowed our way through the mud. Before long, we saw Deputy Kile's car up ahead. He had slipped off the road and gone into the ditch, and the car was pretty seriously stuck.

Slim broke the silence. "How'd you manage to fall into the ditch?"

"I was looking for a missing person. That's what I drove out here to do. My right front wheel slipped into the ditch and that was all she wrote."

"That car's worthless in mud. You should have parked on gravel and walked."

"Am I going to have to listen to your mouth all day?"

"Heck yes. I love it when you mess up. I might even write a story for the newspaper."

The deputy sighed and rubbed me behind the ears. "Hank, you stink but soap and a bath will fix you up. Slim's got problems that soap won't touch."

I agreed and was glad that he had noticed.

Slim had to drive a quarter-mile north to find a place to turn around, then we chugged back to the squad car. He stopped a short distance in front of the car, in a spot where they could hook both vehicles to a tow rope.

It was still pouring rain. The deputy said, "I guess you expect me to hook us up."

"Well, you're the one with the raincoat, and you're the one who brung us to the dance." He noticed the deputy's five-buckle overshoes. "How'd you happen to bring galoshes?"

"Slim, we always go prepared. I carry 'em in the trunk all the time."

"Well, it's too bad you never learned to drive in mud. Hook us up and give me a signal when you're ready. Hang on to your drawers 'cause I'm going to cob this thing and jerk you back in the road. I'll keep pulling till we find some solid ground with gravel. Try not to mess up your clothes."

The deputy laughed and stepped out into the rain. His galoshes sank into the mud.

I hopped up in the seat and watched out the back window. The deputy slogged to his car, opened the trunk, and brought out a twenty-foot nylon tow rope with loops on both ends. He slipped one loop into a towing hook on the front of his car and slipped the other loop over the hitch ball on the pickup.

He got into his car, rolled down the window, and made a circular motion with his left hand. That was the signal.

Slim had been watching in his mirror. "Okay, pooch, hang on."

He jammed the gearshift up into Grandma Low, mashed on the gas, and popped the clutch, but the result wasn't as dramatic as I had expected. Mud. We slithered forward and had a little speed built up when the slack went out of the rope. It gave the car a jerk and we kept moving. Good! I barked.

The car was moving but didn't come out of the ditch. Slim was watching in the mirror and stomped the gas to the floor. The pickup fish-tailed in the road and we were throwing mudballs with all four tires.

Soon, Deputy Kile's hood and windshield were plastered with mud and, well, I guess he couldn't see where he was going. His hand flagged the air, then he stuck his head out the window and yelled.

That was a bad idea, because his face caught several mudballs, and I think one of them might have hit him in the mouth.

Slim was too busy to notice. He gripped the steering wheel with both hands and kept his boot on the gas. We went along this way for a while, with Deputy Kile blind in the ditch and us going sideways down the road and mud flying everywhere, until...oops...our back wheels slipped off into an unusually swampy part of the ditch and then... oops...the front end fell off into the ditch and...

Uh oh. The motor was roaring, the tires were digging holes in the mud, and we came to a stop. Slim threw it in reverse and tried to rock the pickup backwards, but we sank deeper into the mud and didn't move.

Deputy Kile was tapping on the window. Slim rolled it down and growled, "Unhook the stupid rope and I'll get back on the road."

Bobby slipped the loop off the hitch ball and signaled for Slim to hit it. He did. The pickup roared, the tires churned up mud and water, and we sank deeper. Slim turned off the engine and his chin dropped on his chest. "I ain't believing this!"

The deputy opened the passenger-side door and tumbled inside. He was a mess. An eerie silence rolled through the cab. My gaze drifted from one to the other. I couldn't imagine where this would go next.

At last, the deputy broke the deadly silence. "How'd you manage to get in the ditch?"

"Bobby, there's times when a man needs to shut his trap. Plan B flopped. You were right and I was wrong, and I'd just as soon not hear about it for the rest of my life."

"Oh no, I wouldn't do that. You know, I was wrong once myself, years ago, and I still remember how it chewed on my pride. Boy, it really hurt."

"The county pays you a huge salary to figure things out, so what do we do now?"

"Well," his gaze moved out the window, "It appears that we've gotten ourselves in a real mess."

"I already know that and we're supposed to be looking for a missing person."

The deputy nibbled his cheek. "We need a dozer, a motor grader, or a tractor, and we don't have one."

The air inside the cab smelled like, I don't know, dirty socks, I suppose. Not pleasant. And a gloomy silence hung over us. It appeared that our rescue mission had flopped and we would spend the next week living in the pickup. I hoped that Deputy Kile had brought some food because I knew Slim hadn't.

Then Slim's head came up and gleam burned in his eyes. "Wait a second, I just had a brilliant idea." He pulled the talkie-walker from his belt and held it up. "I might find us a tractor, if this thing didn't get ruined in the rain." He pressed a button and said, "Slim to Viola, are you there?"

Silence. We held our breath. "Yes, I'm here. Did you find him?"

"Not yet. We've experienced a few problems."

"Oh dear. What happened?"

"Well, it's a long story, but we've got two vehicles stuck in this hay meadow and they're both buried to the axles."

"Slim, we've got to find Daddy! Mother and I are worried sick."

"Viola, everybody's worried sick. We need your help. Can you drive Woodrow's tractor?"

There was another long silence and everyone in the cab waited to hear what she would say. "Well...I guess so. I've driven it in the field, helping Daddy."

"Good. Do you remember how to start it?"

"I'm not sure. No. Daddy always starts it."

"Okay, listen. It's one of them old-style diesel engines that uses a gasoline starter motor. You start the little motor and let it run for a minute. There's two levers on the left side of the steering wheel. Pull the left one back and hold it, then

67

pull the right one and hold it. When the diesel engine starts up, turn the levers loose and shut off the little motor. And don't forget, that tractor's got a hand clutch, not a foot pedal. It's the big lever to the right of the steering wheel."

Another silence. "Slim, I'll never remember all of that."

"When you get to the barn, call me back and I'll walk you through it. It's time to cowgirl up, kiddo. We need your help on this deal."

"Well...I can try."

"That's my gal. The rain has slacked off some but it's going to be wet on that tractor. Dress for wet weather."

"Will you still love me if my hair's a mess?"

He laughed. "Depends on how bad you look. We'll see about that when you get here. Call me from the barn. Over and out."

Deputy Kile had been listening. "The girl has spunk. And she's going to marry you?"

"That's what people keep saying."

"Poor child. What kind of tractor is that?"

"It's an old John Deere model D, just the kind of antique junk you'd expect Woodrow to have on the place. It was probably the first tractor he ever bought and he's too cheap to buy another one."

"I hope she can get it cranked off. Otherwise, you'll have to walk two miles in the mud and get it yourself."

"Why me? You're the one who started this circus."

The deputy scooted down in the seat and closed his eyes. "I'll be taking a nap. I got called out on a wreck at one o'clock. Wake me up when the fun starts."

Slim wagged his head. "The taxpayers of this county sure don't get much for their money."

The deputy smiled and was soon snoring.

Ten minutes later, Viola called on the whachamcallit and Slim guided her through the process of starting the tractor, which seemed awfully complicated. In fact...okay, maybe I dozed off, but don't forget that I was following the example of Chief Deputy Kile. He wanted everyone on the team to be well-rested and ready for action, don't you see, and I'm a team player.

The next thing I knew, a voice said, "By grabs, she made it, here she comes!"

I leaped to my feet and barked. What was going on around here...and where was here? I blinked my eyes and...hay meadow, rain sizzling down, water standing everywhere, and good grief, someone was coming toward us in a green tractor that was sliding in the road and throwing up wads of mud!

And where was Drover? He had vanished! Hadn't we been on a mission to find the little goof? No, wait, hold everything. Ha ha. Okay, you

probably thought...never mind, skip it. We were in Slim's pickup and Miss Viola had just arrived in the tractor and things were looking brighter.

Now we're cooking and we can cancel the Code Three.

CHAPTER EIGHT

Tractor To the Rescue

This is pretty exciting, isn't it? You bet. I had led my squad of Texas Rangers on a very important Search and Rescue Mission. We had encountered impossible weather conditions and had lost two pieces of motorized equipment in a swamp that pretended to be a hay meadow. We're talking about world-class mud, fellers, the kind of mud you would never expect to find in the Great American Desert.

But I was back in charge and we were fixing to turn things around. I had called for heavy equipment and it had just arrived.

Deputy Kile was napping with his head resting against the fogged-up window. A wicked grin sprang to Slim's mouth. He banged his hand on the dash, blew the horn, and yelled, "Arise and sing, ye slackers of the world, it's time to go to work!"

Heh. That jolted Deputy Kile out of his nap. He sat up straight and blinked his eyes. "Did your mother ever tell you that you were a noisy, obnoxious, unbearable brat?"

"All the time. It didn't do any good. Let's get started. We still have to find Woodrow." He drilled me with his eyes. "You stay in the pickup, Shep."

Yes, but...actually, that sounded pretty good, I mean, the world out there was a real mess. I'm no cupcake but there's a limit on how much mud I can use in one morning. So, yes, I would remain behind the lines and monitor the situation from the Control Center.

My troops braved the elements and stood out in a light rain. Water gushed down the ditches on both sides of the road, the hay meadow had become a shallow lake, and the road had turned to mush.

Viola pulled up in front of the men and jerked back on the hand clutch. The tractor stopped in its tracks...which were pretty deep, even in the middle of the road. She wore a yellow rain slicker, rubber boots, and what appeared to be her daddy's old fishing hat, which was too big and made her ears stick out.

Slim slogged over to the tractor. His hat was

soaked and had lost its cocky cowboy shape. The brim was drooping and it looked more like, I don't know, the hat of a moonshiner, I suppose, than a cowboy's outfit. His shirt was plastered to his skin and bones, but he didn't seem to notice.

He gave Viola his hand and helped her down from the tractor, then gave her a close inspection. "You still look pretty cute but your pony tail got wet and you've got mud on your face." He wiped off a couple of mud spots. "Good job, bringing the tractor. You're a frontier woman for sure." He turned to Deputy Kile. "I'll run the tractor. Get the tow rope and hook us up."

By the time Slim had gotten the tractor backed into position, the deputy was there with the rope. He studied the pickup's bumper for a moment, then motioned for Slim to climb down off the tractor. "You've got this pickup buried so deep, we can't tie on to the frame."

Slim brought a shovel from the bed of the pickup. "I doubt if you remember how to use one of these, so I'll demonstrate. Pay attention." He moved shovelfulls of gummy mud from beneath the pickup's front end, until he had made a pretty big hole.

He was breathing hard but managed to say, "That's my part. You hook it up."

"Thanks a lot."

See, hooking it up meant that Deputy Kile had to lie down in the mud and water, reach under the pickup's front end, and attach the rope to the frame. His poncho kept some of the muck off his clothes, but not all. When he stood up, his pants from the knees-down were caked with mud and so were his hands.

Slim laughed. "Leahwana's going to scalp you."

"She's got a good sharp knife, buddy, and I'll make sure you're on the list. Can you run that tractor without getting stuck? You didn't do so well with a four-wheel drive pickup."

"There's no way to stick a tractor."

"That's what you said about your hot-shot pickup with four-wheel drive and radial tires."

"Tractors don't get stuck."

The deputy wiped his hands on the poncho. "You know what? They do get stuck. I've seen it happen in mud and snow. It's called 'high-center.' When it happens, you call for a dozer. Don't slip off into the ditch because there's no bottom on that mud."

Slim rolled his eyes. "Bobby, this ain't my first rodeo. You run the county, I'll run the tractor."

Miss Viola had been listening. "Do you suppose we could get on with this? Daddy's out there somewhere and we need to find him."

"I agree. Why don't you get in the pickup with Deputy Kile and let's get 'er done."

Viola got into the pickup and, well, that was great news for me. Have I mentioned that she was crazy about me? She was and it was one of those things that just happened on its own, without any effort or planning, like morning dew falling on a yellow cactus flower. The first time our eyes met, she knew I was the dog she'd been waiting for.

After that, well, nothing could come between us, not even Slim and his engagement ring with the microscopic diamond. I mean, she liked the guy, don't get me wrong, and I liked him too, but no matter what he did or how hard he tried, he would never be the Dog of Her Dreams.

That was ME.

When she got into the pickup, my heart raced and my tail began thrashing, and the very instant she closed the door, I dived into her lap, the one place in the universe where I most sincerely wanted to be. It must have startled her and she uttered a little squeak, so naturally I gave her a lick on the cheek. She was the kind of woman who responded to licks on the...

She pushed me away. "Hank, you're wet!"

Huh? Well, of course I was wet. The whole

world was wet. Everything that isn't dry is wet.

"And, frankly, you don't smell so great."

Oh, that hurt! You talk about *crushed*. That was the kind of cutting remark I would expect from Sally May, but not from Miss Viola. And what was the big deal about Wet Dog Smell? Nobody ever complains about Wet People Smell, I mean, Deputy Kile was sitting in the same pickup and he'd been out in the same rain that had fallen

upon the hairs of my back, but she didn't say a word about…

Okay, Deputy Kile hadn't jumped into her lap or licked her cheek, and maybe that made a difference, but the point is that she had rejected me, for the first time ever, and let the record state that my heart was so pulverized, I wasn't sure I would ever recover.

Suddenly the whole world turned dark—dark and gloomy and unbearable. If she couldn't love me as a wet dog, then maybe I'd been wrong about…well, about us, her and me, our relationship. Maybe I was just another dog to her, another mutt with fleas and dandruff and doggie odor who had entered the living room of her life, only to get pitched out the back door.

Is this sad or what? You bet. In fact, I'm not sure I can go on with the story. I mean, who cares if we got the pickup out of the mud and resumed our mission to find Viola's lost daddy?

I guess we could try to limp on. Yes, let's put on a brave face and keep going.

Okay, where were we? Oh yes, in a ranch pickup that was seriously stuck in a muddy hay meadow. Slim was ready to put some thunder into the effort with a big diesel tractor that could claw its way through any kind of mud.

He pushed the throttle lever as far as it would go and a puff of black smoke spurted out of the exhaust pipe. He rammed the clutch lever home and the big tractor tires began spinning and throwing mudballs everywhere.

The slack went out of the tow rope and the pickup got a jerk. Deputy Kile clenched his teeth together and floor-boarded the pickup. Hey, we were moving! This was going to work.

But wait. We were moving forward, all right, but the pickup stayed in the ditch. We needed to get OUT of the ditch, right? Because the ditch was full of water and a bunch of it was coming over the hood and splashing on the windshield.

In fact, we were stone blind, trying to see through muddy water, so Deputy Kile turned on the windshield wipers and now we could see that...uh oh...the weight of the pickup appeared to be making the tractor to run sideways in the road and, well, was causing it to drift toward the ditch.

But that would never happen, right? Everyone involved in this mission knew that the entire hay meadow had become a bottomless swamp and the only safe place to be was in the road.

I cut a glance at Miss Viola, the stone-hearted woman who had recently tossed me aside like a dirty sock. She was staring straight ahead, her mouth half-open. She was worried. I turned to Deputy Kile. He had little drops of sweat on his upper lip and muttered, "Keep it out of the ditch, cowboy."

You know, fresh mud is very slippery and spinning tires can cause a tractor to drift in the direction of the object that's being pulled. The object being pulled was a heavy ranch pickup... and you'll never guess what happened.

You'd better keep reading.

CHAPTER NINE

Unbelievable

Okay, let's get on with this.

There we were in the pickup, crashing through a ditch filled with muddy brown water and Deputy Kile had it running wide open in four-wheel drive. We were being dragged by Slim Chance on the tractor. The tractor tires were grinding away on the road and throwing up incredible chunks of mud that were raining down on Slim's hat and the fenders of the tractor.

The three of us in the cab watched with wide eyes as the back wheels of the tractor moved closer and closer to the edge of the road. Surely, he wouldn't...the right rear wheel slipped off the road and fell into the ditch, but Slim kept grinding away at full throttle and mud kept flying.

The left rear tire of the tractor left the road and slid into the ditch.

Gulp.

The tractor's front end slid into the ditch.

We slowed to a crawl. The tractor tires were grinding away, slinging mud and water, but we were hardly moving.

We weren't moving at all. Our forward progress had stopped.

I heard a voice to my left, Deputy Kile. "He's high-centered."

A creepy silence fell over us. Deputy Kile heaved a deep breath and shut off the pickup motor. Slim yanked the hand clutch and throttle lever, and the tractor tires stopped churning mud. He draped his arms over the steering wheel and rested his forehead on his arms. His hat was decorated with mudballs.

Miss Viola's eyes darted around. "What does this mean?"

The deputy hacked a kind of laugh. "It means we're out of business, shut down, skunked. We don't have any equipment left to get stuck. Against incredible odds, we've managed to disable a police cruiser, a four-wheel drive pickup, and a tractor. We've turned a search-and-rescue mission into a Three Stooges comedy."

"Oh dear. What's next?"

"Well, I'll probably get fired. And Slim? I can't even imagine. Maybe he'll become a Trappist monk. They've got a monastery in Kentucky. Maybe he can hide his past and they'll let him in."

Viola drew a big breath of air. "Oh dear."

Time throbbed. I thought about crawling into Viola's lap, I mean, this was a difficult time for all of us and she needed...but no, she'd already tossed me into the Trash Heap of Life. Why? *Because I smelled like a wet dog!*

Never mind that sometimes a dog gets wet. Never mind that a wet dog is SUPPOSED to smell like a wet dog. Never mind that...wait, hold everything. Would you believe that Drover and I had once done a song on this very subject? It's true, several years ago. It took the form of a debate between the two of us, I mean a heavy-duty discussion on the very important subject of Dog Odor.

Awesome song. Normally I hate to repeat my songs repeat my songs, but this subject is SO important and the song addresses the issue SO well, I think we need to make an exception.

Hang on, let's give it a listen and pay special attention to the words.

A Dog Should Smell Like a Dog

Hank [Melody One]
Drover, a hog should smell like a hog.
A frog should smell like a frog.
A dog should smell like a...what?

Drover
Well, a dog...I guess.
Hank
Sing with me now

Hank and Drover [Melody One]
A hog should smell like a hog.
      (A hog should smell like a hog)
A frog should smell like a frog.
      (A frog should smell like a frog)
A dog should smell like a dog.
      (A dog should smell like a dog)

Hank
Naturally. Do you get it now?

Hank [Melody Two]
A bee should smell like a bee.
      (I don't like bees)
A tree should smell like a tree.

(I can't climb trees)
And I should smell just like me.
Naturally.
     (I'm not so sure about that)

Drover [Melody One]
Yeah, but *natural* is more than you think.
     (What did you say?)
Your argument's developed a kink.
     (What does that mean?)
The problem is just that you stink,
     (Oh brother!)
Naturally.
     (Drover...)

Hank [Melody Two]
Something is wrong with your nose.
     (I don't think so)
What if I smelled like a rose?
     (You ought to try it)
What if I painted my toes?
     (I never said that you should)
Unnatural, that's what it would be.

Duet

Hank [Melody Two]	**Drover [Melody One]**
A hog should smell like a hog	*Natural* is not what you think
A frog should smell like a frog.	Your argument's developed a kink.
A dog should smell like a dog,	The problem is just that you stink,
Naturally.	Naturally.
Everything's going to work out,	This thing will never work out,
Naturally.	Naturally.

There you are. Is that a great song or what?

A DOG SHOULD SMELL LIKE A DOG! It's part of God's plan for the earth and the solar system. What kind of screwy world would this be if a wet dog smelled like a dry dog? It would be totally unnatural. Clocks would run sideways, birds would fly backwards, and cats would be in charge.

Is that the kind of world Viola wanted?

Oh well. Eventually I would get over the hurt and the pain and the painful hurt, but for now, my life was in scrambles. In *shambles*, I guess it should be. My life was in shambles and the only good thing I could see was that the rain had quit and the clouds were starting to break up.

Maybe a few sunbeams would nurse me back to health and restore a tiny sense of hope to my shattered life. Oh, what a fool I'd been, thinking that she really cared about me and that we were Tight For Life, like salt and pepper and eggs and bacon!

Well, we were finished. Once a dog has been spurned...

"Hank?"

Huh?

Was that a woman's voice? I turned my tear-soaked gaze to the right. She seemed to be looking at...well, at me.

"Come here." She patted her lap with a soft hand that was speckled with mud.

Me? No. It wasn't that simple.

"Come on."

No. It was over between us.

"Oh, come here."

Would I...could I...okay, maybe one last time. She needed me. One last time.

I crept into her warm lap and didn't lick her on the face. This was a new beginning and we needed to go slow, rebuild everything from the ground up. I felt her fingers rubbing around my ears. I melted and became a puddle of hair.

I was still a wet dog who smelled like wet dog, but SHE DIDN'T CARE!

My life was restored, oh happy day!

But then I became aware that Slim had climbed off the tractor and was standing beside the pickup—and by the way, he was standing in ditch water that came over the tops of his boots. In other words, his boots must have been full of water.

Deputy Kile rolled down the window. In normal times, those two would have started snarling and snapping at each other, each blaming the other for this...this incredible mess we were in. But not this time. The incredible mess had become so incredible, they were speechless and had been reduced to normal behavior.

Slim's face wore the expression of a beaten man and he spoke in a low, straight tone. "We'd better go on foot and try to find Woodrow."

The deputy nodded. "I agree."

"Viola, you might as well stay in the pickup."

"Forget that."

"There's no need..."

"Slim, I'm going."

"Well, okay. I hope y'all can get out of the pickup. The water's up to the floorboard."

Deputy Kile looked down at his feet. "Yeah, it's already covered the floor mat. See if you can open the door."

Slim pulled open the door, causing waves, and the deputy stepped out in the water that was over the tops of his boots. He cringed as the cold water oozed down to his ankles, and he slogged to higher ground.

Slim waded around to Viola's side and told her

to crawl out the window. "I'll carry you to the road so you won't get soaked."

That brought a little smile. "How noble!"

"It's the Cowboy Way, ma'am. I need to do something to redeem myself."

"I weigh more than you think."

"I ain't scared."

She crawled out the window and settled into his arms. I followed, diving out the window, into the water. She stroked his wet hair with her fingers and looked into his eyes. "We should do this more often."

He laughed and started slogging toward the road. Was I jealous? Maybe. A little. Yes. But she and I had patched things up and, after all, she was engaged to the guy. It was okay.

Slim slogged several steps through the water, carrying the prettiest, sweetest gal in all of Texas, when...oops...his boot got bogged in the mud and...you won't believe this...they both went crashing into the water!

I held my breath and waited for Slim to explode in a screaming wall-eyed fit. I mean, this had turned into one of the worst days of his life and now...well, he had dumped his fiancée into a ditch and she was sitting in muddy water up to her ribs.

The morning air became deadly quiet, then...

Viola started laughing...and Slim started laughing and up on the road, Deputy Kile cackled and yelled, "That ain't the way Roy and Gene would have done it!"

Slim got to his feet and pulled Viola to her feet and they staggered their way up to the road. There, all three of them sat down in the mud, pulled off their boots, and poured out enough water to support a couple of goldfish.

They got to their feet and Slim said, "Let's go find Woodrow."

CHAPTER TEN

I Find Him

Nobody on our team wanted to talk about all the bad things that might have happened to the old gentleman, but everyone was thinking about it. The lighthearted mood we'd experienced when Slim dumped his girlfriend into the water gave way to a more somber atmosphere.

We started walking down the road toward Woodrow's pickup, slogging and sliding through mud. Everyone's boots and my feet were caked with the stuff but nobody said anything about it. We had moved beyond comment or complaint. Our world had turned into a gigantic mud pen and we just had to live with it.

The sun broke through the clouds, and its warm rays chased away some of the chill in our bones. I mean, rain water is *cold* and we'd all had plenty of exposure to it. The sunshine felt good and all at once we had ourselves a beautiful morning: crystal clean air, warm yellow sun, grass and trees that were green beyond green, water standing in every low spot and cow track, and a whole Milky Way of wildflowers splashed across the pasture—red, yellow, orange, blue, purple, and white.

You talk about delicious smells in the air! Nobody was grumbling about so-called Wet Dog Smell, because we were breathing the perfume of thirty different varieties of wildflower, plus the blooms of wild grapes, which might have been the sweetest of all.

It might have gone down as the prettiest morning the world had ever seen, except for the fact that we weren't there to smell the posies or admire the colors. We were on a serious search-and-rescue mission.

Had you forgotten that? You need to sit up straight and pay attention. Viola's daddy had wandered off and we had to find him.

At last we arrived at Woodrow's pickup. Everyone was out of breath from dragging mud-heavy boots through the mud. Hey, even I was panting for air and I wasn't wearing boots. After a short rest, Deputy Kile studied the inside of the pickup, then knelt down and looked at the ground.

"He didn't get stuck. He stopped on the side of the road and left his vehicle. Why? Do y'all have any cattle in this pasture?"

Viola shook her head. "No. We won't turn cattle in here until we cut the hay."

"So he wasn't looking at a new calf or a sick cow. You don't suppose he got out to look at the wildflowers, do you?"

She smiled. "No. That's not something he would do."

The deputy pushed himself up to a standing position. "He stopped the pickup, turned off the motor, got out, and started walking. Slim, you said his tracks went north?"

"Yep, toward that grove of cottonwoods."

"Well, let's spread out in a line and walk north."

Slim finger-kicked a wad of mud off the brim of his hat. "Had you thought of calling out his name?"

The deputy's eyes flicked back and forth. "I was just fixing to say that. On the count of three, we'll yell out his name. One, two, three."

And they all yelled, "WOOD-DROW!"

I didn't yell his name but I barked. It was a good one too.

We listened and heard...birds chirping, so we did it again. We stood very still and strained our ears and heard chirping birds.

Deputy Kile hitched up his pants. "Okay, let's spread out and start walking, ten yards apart. Move slow and look for something he might have dropped, a piece of thread on a bush, tracks, anything. Holler out if you see something."

And so the search began. I just happened to find myself beside Miss Viola. Okay, it wasn't an accident, I planned it that way. Who would want to trudge through mud, weeds, and brush beside Slim Chance or Deputy Kile? Not me. I was doing volunteer work and I could walk with anyone with whom I chose to walk with whom.

See, she needed me to protect her from snakes and badgers. And skunks. There might be a skunk hiding in those tall weeds, I mean you don't always see them, and she might step right in the middle of one. I would be out front in the scout position, ready to take a hit for her.

Heh. If that happened, we might have another discussion of Dog Odor.

So, yes, I took the lead and we plunged into the tall weeds and grass, and they were very tall and wet. No problem. I had a first-class nose working the trail and...

Huh?

Did you see what I saw? Maybe not, because you weren't there, but unless my eyes were playing tricks on me...THERE WAS A MAN UP AHEAD OF US, WALKING OUR WAY!

Holy smokes, you talk about cold chills skating down your backbone! I got a whole stampede of cold chills and when I tried to blast out a warning bark, it...well, came out as a squeak.

He wore red suspenders on khaki pants that bagged in the seat and had a thatch of white hair on his...on his head, of course, and maybe that was obvious. He walked along with his eyes on the ground.

Wait, hold everything! You don't suppose... could this possibly be Woodrow? I reloaded the artillery and fired off another bark, this time a big one, huge, with echoes and everything.

Viola saw him too. She stopped in her tracks and let out a squeal. "Daddy! Boys, I've found him, he's over here!"

Actually, I had found him and that's the main reason every search-and-rescue needs a dog—not just any dog but a highly trained, highly skilled blue-ribbon, top-of-the-line cowdog. But if Viola wanted to say she found him, hey, that was all right, I mean, we were part of the same team and the guy was her daddy, not mine.

As you might expect, things began happening pretty fast. Deputy Kile and Slim came at a trot, and all three of them rushed over to Woodrow and surrounded him.

Viola threw her arms around him. "Daddy, we've been worried sick about you! Are you all right? Where on earth have you been?"

Woodrow didn't look like a man who was sick or wounded, but he didn't answer and he wasn't wet and his clothes weren't even muddy. He looked like a man who was in a bad mood and wished we would all go away...which I thought was pretty weird. I mean, the rest of us looked like refugees, because we'd spent the last I-don't-know-how long getting three vehicles stuck in the mud so we could go looking for HIM.

Now we'd found him and his face expressed all the excitement of a prune.

Viola studied him. "Daddy? Can you talk?"

He aimed a finger at Slim. "I ain't talking to him." His finger swung around and pointed to Deputy Kile. "And I ain't talking to him. I'll talk to you. Come on."

He started walking toward his pickup. Viola shrugged and gave her head a bewildered shake. "I don't know what's going on but maybe I can find out." She followed her daddy to the pickup

and they got inside.

Deputy Kile slapped a mosquito on his neck. "What got his tail in the ringer?"

"I don't know."

"Did you do something to make him mad?"

"Well, I was born and that ticked him off, then I got engaged to his daughter. I'm not sure he'll ever forgive me for that."

"Well, he's got a point, but she seems to like you. That ought to count for something."

"Ought to, but you know how daddies are. No man's good enough for their daughter."

"It might help if you owned a big ranch and a few dozen oil wells."

Slim chuckled. "I hadn't thought of that. Good idea."

Ho hum. We waited. The men found sticks and cleaned some of the mud off their boots. And swatted mosquitoes. The hateful things had prospered in the wet spring and the pleasant morning brought them out in swarms. Mosquitoes seem dedicated to the idea that no pleasant day should go unpunished.

At last we heard the pickup door open and shut, and every eye locked on Miss Viola. She was walking toward us, holding her hat and wearing a peculiar expression. The men climbed to their feet and tried to control their curiosity. I mean, she was taking her sweet time and we were all dying to know what was going on.

She finally joined our little circle and motioned for us to follow her. We did, moving away from the pickup. She stopped and threw a glance over her shoulder. In a soft but firm voice she said, "This is the craziest story I ever heard. You must promise not to laugh."

Slim and the deputy exchanged glances and said, "Okay."

You don't know what she was fixing to tell us, but I do and it was...well, you'll see.

The Craziest
Story You
Ever Heard

Okay, I was there and heard the whole thing. As a matter of fact, I made careful notes of her entire testimony. I don't suppose we have time to review my notes, do we? Really? Okay, if you're sure about that, I'll open the case file.

The Viola File
June Somethingth of Some Year
Recorded by Hank the Cowdog
Head of the Ranch's Security Division

[On the morning of whatever day it was, Miss Viola gave the following testimony to the Head of Ranch Security, witnessed by Chief Deputy Kile and Slim Chance, hired hand, in a flooded hay

101

meadow on the Woodrow Ranch, while all parties swatted mosquitoes].

Around 6:00 a.m., Woodrow finished his coffee and left the house. He paused at the yard gate to check the rain gauge. It contained one dead fly and three gnats. He dumped them out and looked up at the sky. He saw nothing that suggested rain.

He walked to his pickup, popped the hood, and fished out the dipstick. He held it close to his eyes and saw that it showed "Full." It had showed Full yesterday, the day before, two days before, the week before, and the month before, but he checks it every morning, just in case.

He slammed the hood, wiped his hands on the seat of his pants, started the pickup, and began driving his pastures, which he did yesterday, the day before, and almost every day of his adult life.

As always, he noticed every tiny detail. The grass was still holding its green and in several spots, it had grown half an inch in the night.

Three whitetail does were grazing weeds in the west meadow. They threw up their tails and ran when they saw the pickup.

A badger crossed the road.

The wooden windmill in the Upper South pasture wasn't making water and needed new leathers. He made a mental note to call Benny and Jake and tell them to come fix it. The salt block beside the windmill was just about used up. Nearby, a cow was nursing a fresh calf. Both looked fine.

The wire gate into the Lower South pasture was sagging. It needed work.

The stock tank in the Lower South contained a dead buzzard, drowned while trying to get a drink. With water standing in all the slews on both sides of the creek, why did a buzzard need to drink out of the stock tank...and get himself drowned? Woodrow fished the dead buzzard out of the tank.

The grass in the hay meadow was looking good. In July, the slews would dry up and he would call Rudolph, the hay man, to start swathing and baling. This year's hay crop promised to be a dandy...if the meadow dried out.

It was then that he noticed the tide of white-capped clouds advancing from the north. They looked pretty threatening. He hadn't listened to the weather. Were the weather wizards predicting rain? It didn't matter. They were usually wrong anyway. He wondered why anyone bothered listening to a weather report that said "50% chance of rain."

There was a 50% chance that pigs would start

wearing lipstick. There was a 50% chance that nothing would ever happen, anywhere, ever.

He continued driving through the meadow and noticed a spot covered with red and orange flowers, Indian blankets. They had popped up overnight and were releasing a powerful smell— not bad but not exactly sweet either. It made his nose itch and he felt a sneeze coming on.

He exercised discipline and resisted the sneeze. This was *his* body and *his* nose, and he didn't want to sneeze. Sneezing got his sinuses stirred up and made his nose run. He chased away several sneezes but one finally got him.

He felt it coming and stopped the pickup on the side of the road. He didn't want to blow snot all over the windshield, so he pointed his face out the window. His eyes sagged shut and his breath quivered, then air rushed into his chest and he exploded. It was a boomer, three sneezes rolled into one.

AAAAAAA-CHOOOOOOO!!

It was one of the biggest sneezes he'd ever produced. He wiped his eyes on a blue polka dot bandana that he always carried in his left hip pocket, across from the wallet he always carried in his right hip pocket, and honked his nose. In fact, he honked it three times.

He had just stuffed the bandana back into his right hip pocket when he was seized by an uneasy feeling. Something wasn't right. The violent sneeze seemed to have changed something important in his life.

Then it struck him. The sneeze had *blown his false teeth out the window*! It was a dental plate he wore to replace two upper incisors, knocked out years ago when he slammed a ballpeen hammer against a pickup tire and it came back and hit him in the mouth, one of the dumbest stunts he'd ever pulled.

He was horrified that he'd blown his teeth out the window. Not only had that dental plate cost him a tub of money, but he was very self-conscious about that gap in his mouth. He didn't want anyone to see him looking like a Halloween pumpkin. He didn't even want to see himself that way.

He HAD to find those teeth!

He stepped out of the pickup and began searching every inch of the ground. It had to be there somewhere, but he couldn't find it. He began sweating and of course his nose was still running, but he didn't take the time to blow it. He felt a rising sense of panic. Then...

This he could not believe. He saw his high-dollar dental plate...IN THE BEAK OF A

ROADRUNNER! The idiot bird must have thought it was a lizard and scooped it up, and now he was twisting his head around and staring at Woodrow with those big, weird, roadrunner eyes.

"Give me back my teeth!" He made a dive for the bird who, naturally, took off running. That's what roadrunners do, even when they're not stealing false teeth, and they're good at running.

In high school, Woodrow was a pretty good athlete. He ran the anchor-leg of Twitchell's sprint relay team, but today he was sixty years past his prime as a sprinter. Even so, he lit a shuck after that bird. He ran until his legs turned to rubber and he was slap out of breath. He stopped to rest.

And it started raining.

He would never get his teeth back!

He didn't have the strength to run to the pickup and noticed a big calf feeder standing in the pasture, only fifty feet to the west. It was a device made of sheet metal and angle-iron, big enough to hold a thousand pounds of creep feed. It had a trough on the south side, covered with a metal overhang. It would be protected from the rain and wind.

He hobbled to the feeder and crawled into the south trough, just as the rain hit. It roared and

poured sheets and buckets of rain. He stayed cozy and dry in his little cabin in the woods, but bored out of his mind.

There was nothing to do but wait. And wait. And brood. He knew his wife and daughter would be worried about him but there wasn't a thing he could do about it. He hoped they wouldn't be silly enough to go looking for him...or, for Pete's sake, to call the neighbors so they could tear up his roads and get their vehicles stuck in the mud.

Then he thought of something even worse. Surely they wouldn't call the sheriff's department... but of course they would! Oh, that's just what he needed, a bunch of Johnny Laws poking around and taking his blood pressure and asking him what happened. And what was he supposed to tell them?

He sneezed and blew his dental plate out the window and a roadrunner ran off with it?

Well, he had news for them. He didn't need their help, he didn't need to be rescued by a bunch of overgrown Boy Scouts, and most of all, he didn't want anyone to see him without his teeth.

And by grabs, he wouldn't! If anybody showed up, he wouldn't talk to them. They could go jump in the lake.

Well, he might talk to Viola. She'd seen him without his teeth and she was his daughter. It was just a shame she was on track to marry a pauper. The girl deserved better.

He listened to the rain and made his plans. When the rain quit, he would high-ball it into town, sneak in the back door of Dr. Allen's office, and get measured for a new upper plate. If he saw anyone he knew, he would cover his mouth with his hand.

Or tell them to shove off. He didn't need friends anyway. They were too much trouble.

And that's where things stood when he heard three voices and a dog howling his name. He was mad. The fools! Why didn't they go away, mind their own business, and leave him alone!

He crawled out of the feeder, madder than a rattlesnake, and started walking to his pickup. When he saw the cop and the cowboy, he wished he'd been armed with a pitchfork. He would have loved to chase them off the ranch, poking their hip pockets with the tines of a fork.

He didn't speak to the men but did pour out his story to Viola, and she told it to us and I got it all down in my report.

End of Case File Viola
Please Destroy at once!

CHAPTER TWELVE

Where Did the Teeth Go?

Wow.

Can you believe that? Viola was right when she said it was the craziest story she'd ever heard. It might have been the craziest story anybody had ever heard.

I can testify that it didn't take Slim and Deputy Kile long to break their Vows of No Laughing. When she got to the part about the old man sneezing his teeth out the window, they were howling—and so was Viola. She could hardly go on with the story. When she came to the part about the roadrunner, it stopped the show. The guys went to the ground laughing, I mean they were on hands and knees, while Viola leaned against a tree trunk, bit her lower lip, and tried to show some restraint.

It was obvious why she wanted to move us away from the pickup. Woodrow was inside, pouting, and she didn't want to get him stirred up with crowd noise.

It took the guys several minutes to unwind their laughter. Finally Slim said, "That's amazing, and it sounds so Woodrow. It couldn't have happened to anybody else."

She placed her hands on her hips and drew in a big breath of air. "That's my daddy, for better or worse. He's just who he is."

"Well, we've had our fun for the day. What do we do now?"

Viola smiled and shrugged. "I don't have the slightest idea. Well, yes I do. Daddy is determined, and I mean DETERMINED, to drive into town and order new teeth, and he's not going to talk to anyone but me. Can we drive his pickup to the house without getting stuck?"

Deputy Kile said, "If Slim's driving, we'll get stuck, I guarantee it. If there's a bog hole anywhere in the county, he'll drive into it."

Slim rolled his eyes. "Here we go again. Bobby, you're the one who started this whole disaster, showing up out here in a two-bit cop car that would get stuck if a cow peed in the road."

The deputy chuckled and spoke to Viola. "I think we can make it to the house. The rain has quit and the sun's drying the road and his pickup has four-wheel drive."

"Well, we'd better go, before he drives off without us and makes us walk."

They started walking south. I had been lying on the ground, which meant that on raising myself to a standing position, I went into a Standard Body Stretch. It's a normal procedure and we always do it. We strike a wide stance, don't you see, with front and rear paws spread far apart, throw a downward curve into the spinalary region and a curl in the tail, open the mouth wide, extend the tongue, and process a big, deep yawn.

It's a pretty complicated procedure, if you want to know the truth, and some dogs do it better than others. I'm pretty good at it. Actually, it's kind of amazing that...

I stopped in the middle of the procedure. My eyes had picked up a tiny glint of white coming from a place where there shouldn't have been a tiny glint of white, in the lower branches of a wild plum bush.

What could it be? I barked. My friends walked on, paying no attention to me.

Okay, I would have to check it out on my own.

I moved toward the spot, slowly and carefully, just in case...well, we never know, could be a skunk or a rattlesnake.

I got a good close look. It wasn't a skunk or a rattlesnake. It was...you know what? It looked like TWO TEETH sitting in a wild plum bush. Well, that was ridiculous. Teeth don't grow on wild plum bushes. Teeth grow in mouths and plum bushes don't have one.

False alarm. In my line of work, we deal with Reality and believe what we see with our own two eyes. If something appears to be impossible and ridiculous, it's impossible and ridiculous, and we don't waste any time with it. That which can't happen doesn't happen, because it can't. Period.

Wild plum bushes don't have teeth.

I spun around and trotted to catch up with my team.

You probably think that I had overlooked something important, right? Go ahead and admit it. You think I had stumbled onto a clue that would bust the case wide open but walked away from it.

Well, okay, maybe I did, but then I got to thinking. Two teeth in a plum bush? Hadn't we been talking about teeth? You don't suppose...

Holy smokes, I whirled around and raced back... which bush was it? My gaze swept the whole area, every bush and weed, but I couldn't find it!

"Hank, come on! Train's fixing to leave!"

Oh no! I had found the missing teeth but had lost them again!

But then...THERE THEY WERE! The dumb bird had parked them in a plum bush. I rushed to the spot and switched on Nosetory Scanners. The report came back in seconds and showed an unmistakable Woodrow Signature.

I had found the missing dental plate!

I gathered it up in the loving embrace of my

powerful jaws and walked as fast as I dared toward the pickup, I mean, I didn't want to mess this up. When I reached the pickup, Slim and Deputy Kile were sitting on the tail gate, apparently because Woodrow didn't want them to see him without his teeth and was making them ride in the back.

Miss Viola was just getting into the cab. I dashed to her before she got the door shut.

She was surprised to see me. "Hank, you'd better ride in the back with the men. You're a mudball." I didn't move and noticed that her eyes seemed to have locked on the object in my mouth. Maybe she thought I had grown buck teeth or something. Anyway, her eyebrows flew up, her mouth dropped open, and she squealed, "Oh my word! Oh my word! Daddy, Hank found your teeth!"

The men came at a gallop and suddenly I was surrounded by a whole crowd of admirers, I mean, this was a dog's dream of the Perfect Life, made even more perfect because one face in the crowd belonged to a lady who adored me.

I had saved her daddy's false teeth and become the Dog of Her Dreams, her hero. We could run away to the mountains and rent a castle with a huge fireplace and live happily ever-afterly and maybe mail a postcard to Slim, back at the ranch.

Be still my heart!

Okay, that wasn't likely to happen, I mean, she was engaged to the guy, but I had definitely scored some big points and had moved into first place as the Dog of Her Dreams. Drover never had much of a chance, but now he was even no chancer.

She lifted the teeth from my mouth, held them up to her shining eyes, and handed them to Woodrow—who was actually smiling! When was the last time that happened? Had anyone in the county ever seen him smile before? Well, he was smiling now and everyone present got a quick look at the gap in his uppers, but it was very brief. He turned away from the audience and when he showed himself again, he had his full smile.

Viola said, "Daddy, you should have cleaned it before you put it in your mouth."

"Sugar, a little dog drool never killed anyone, might even be good for the colon." He reached across the cab and patted my head. "Good dog. Me and you have cheated Dr. Allen out of five hundred bucks and you can ride in my pickup any time you want. Get in here and ride up front. Come on!"

Really? Wow. I was amazed. I leaped up, crossed Viola's lap, and took my position between them. Guess who had to ride in the back with the feed sacks, bailing wire, and two cedar posts.

Slim and Deputy Kile! Hee hee, I loved it.

Oh, by the way, Viola didn't say a word about Wet Dog Smell. So there!

Woodrow put the pickup into four-wheel drive and we started back to the house. The pickup slipped and slid, but the old man took his time and kept 'er in the middle of the road. His expression darkened when we came to the tractor and pickup, both buried in the mud.

"Which genius was responsible for that mess?"

"All of us. One thing led to another."

"I hope that boyfriend of yours knows something about horses, 'cause he don't know beans about driving a tractor."

"Daddy, we were out here looking for *you*. And he's not my boyfriend. We're engaged."

"Yeah, I heard that. It'll take me a week to get that tractor cleaned up. I hope he didn't burn up the clutch."

She looked at me and shook her head. Yes, I understood.

When we made it back to the house, Viola's mom was thrilled to see us. She was waiting on the porch, with little Mister Half-Stepper curled up at her feet, and she gave the old man a hug. Viola told her the story of our adventures and she laughed so hard she had to sit down.

Woodrow stood nearby, shaking his head and scowling. I guess he'd filled his quota of smiles for the month.

Meanwhile, Deputy Kile went into the house and used the phone. He called the sheriff's office and they located a dozer in the area. Half an hour later, a big semi-truck pulled up at the house, with a muddy D-5 dozer chained and boomered down on a flatbed trailer. The driver undid the chains and backed the dozer down the ramps. White letters on the truck's door said "Scot Erickson Trucking."

Deputy Kile talked Woodrow into loaning us his pickup (it was the only vehicle on the ranch that wasn't buried in mud) and we led the dozer to the first vehicle, Deputy Kile's squad car. It was an easy fix. Scot snatched it out of the mud with his winch line and the deputy parked it on a dry spot in the road.

We moved on to the other two. Slim had to wade ditch water to get into his pickup and found two inches of standing water on the floorboard, but the winch had no problem pulling him back on the road. The tractor wasn't so easy, I mean, when you get a tractor stuck, you've got a serious mud problem, but Scot got 'er done.

It took two hours, from start to finish, but we

finally made it back to the house with all the vehicles. Scot loaded the dozer and chained it down, then shook hands with Slim and Deputy Kile. He was smiling and very friendly and handed out business cards.

"I'll send you boys a box of cheese at Christmas. We sure appreciate your business and I want to stay in touch. Next time you do something stupid, give me a call." As he was walking to his truck, he threw his arms into the air and yelled, "Yes, Lord, send us more mud!"

He blew his air horn and drove off in a big puff of black diesel smoke. Slim watched with a sour expression. "He's kind of a smart-aleck, ain't he."

"He's got a warped sense of humor. He's pulled me out before."

"Well, I hope you enjoy your Christmas cheese, 'cause you've blown my work day to smithereens, and I haven't even started washing Woodrow's tractor."

The deputy glanced at his watch. "Sorry I can't stick around to help, but I need to check things at the office."

"Thanks, Bobby, I expected no less."

"Any time. We're here to serve." He reached down and rubbed my ears. "Hank, you saved the day. Nice work. I'll bet Woodrow wishes you were the one engaged to his daughter."

Slim snorted a laugh, but you know what? The same thought had crossed my mind. Too bad it would never happen. Sigh.

Deputy Kile drove back to town and Slim went to work, hosing mud off of the tractor, with Woodrow standing right there, giving helpful advice. It was the middle of the afternoon before we got away and went back to work on the ranch, and that's about the end of the story.

The Case of the Missing Teeth had been one of the toughest investigations of my whole career. I mean, who would have dreamed that a roadrunner would turn out to be a denture thief? And who would have thought he would stash the loot in a wild plum bush?

Even Deputy Kile missed the clues, but maybe he picked up a few tips, working with me. I'm always glad to help local law enforcement. The toughest part of the job is staying humble. It's a real challenge and I have to work at it every day.

Anyway, this case is closed.

Have you read all
of Hank's adventures?

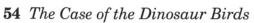

Finding Hank

The Most-Often Asked Questions about Hank the Cowdog

For more than 35 years, John R. Erickson has entertained three generations of readers with Hank the Cowdog's hilarious antics, and now, for the first time, in this beautiful, full-color volume, he answers the most common questions he has received from fans over the years!

Written in an engaging question-and answer style, this collector's item — complete with illustrations and original photographs — provides a unique behind-the-scenes look at the people, places, and real-life animals and incidents behind your favorite Hank stories!

And, be sure to check out the Audiobooks!

If you've never heard a *Hank the Cowdog* audiobook, you're missing out on a lot of fun! Each Hank book has also been recorded as an unabridged audiobook for the whole family to enjoy!

Praise for the Hank Audiobooks:

"It's about time the Lone Star State stopped hogging Hank the Cowdog, the hilarious adventure series about a crime solving ranch dog. Ostensibly for children, the audio renditions by author John R. Erickson are sure to build a cult following among adults as well." — *Parade Magazine*

"Full of regional humor . . . vocals are suitably poignant and ridiculous. A wonderful yarn." — *Booklist*

"For the detectin' and protectin' exploits of the canine Mike Hammer, hang Hank's name right up there with those of other anthropomorphic greats...But there's no sentimentality in Hank: he's just plain more rip-roaring fun than the others. Hank's misadventures as head of ranch security on a spread somewhere in the Texas Panhandle are marvelous situation comedy." — *School Library Journal*

"Knee-slapping funny and gets kids reading."

— *Fort Worth Star Telegram*

The Ranch Life Learning Series

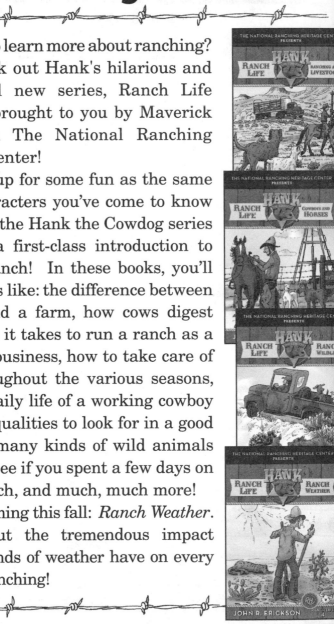

Want to learn more about ranching? Check out Hank's hilarious and educational new series, Ranch Life Learning, brought to you by Maverick Books and The National Ranching Heritage Center!

Saddle up for some fun as the same cast of characters you've come to know and love in the Hank the Cowdog series gives you a first-class introduction to life on a ranch! In these books, you'll learn things like: the difference between a ranch and a farm, how cows digest grass, what it takes to run a ranch as a successful business, how to take care of cattle throughout the various seasons, what the daily life of a working cowboy looks like, qualities to look for in a good horse, the many kinds of wild animals you might see if you spent a few days on Hank's ranch, and much, much more!

And, coming this fall: *Ranch Weather*. Learn about the tremendous impact different kinds of weather have on every aspect of ranching!

Love Hank's Hilarious Songs?

Hank the Cowdog's "Greatest Hits" albums bring together the music from the unabridged audiobooks you know and love! These wonderful collections of hilarious (and sometimes touching) songs are unmatched. Where else can you learn about coyote philosophy, buzzard lore, why your dog is protecting an old corncob, how bugs compare to hot dog buns, and much more!

And, be sure to visit Hank's "Music Page" on the official website to listen to some of the songs and download FREE Hank the Cowdog ringtones!

"Audio-Only" Stories

Ever wondered what those "Audio-Only" Stories in Hank's Official Store are all about?

The Audio-Only Stories are Hank the Cowdog adventures that have never been released as books. They are about half the length of a typical Hank book, and there are currently seven of them. They have run as serial stories in newspapers for years and are now available as audiobooks!

Teacher's Corner

Know a teacher who uses Hank in their classroom? You'll want to be sure they know about Hank's "Teacher's Corner"! Just click on the link on the homepage, and you'll find free teacher's aids, such as a printable map of Hank's ranch, a reading log, coloring pages, blog posts specifically for teachers and librarians, and much more!

The following activities are samples from *The Hank Times*, the official newspaper of Hank's Security Force. Please do not write on these pages unless this is your book. And, even then, why not just find a scrap of paper?

"Photogenic" Memory Quiz

We all know that Hank has a "photogenic" memory—being aware of your surroundings is an important quality for a Head of Ranch Security. Now *you* can test your powers of observation.

How good is your memory? Look at the illustration on page 27 and try to remember as many things about it as possible. Then turn back to this page and see how many questions you can answer.

1. Was Slim holding his hat with HIS Left or Right hand?

2. Were there clouds in the sky?

3. Was Hank's back foot on the Bottom, Middle, or Top step?

4. How many pockets on Slim's shirt? 0, 1 or 2?

5. Which of Slim's feet was in the air? HIS Left or Right?

6. How many of Hank's ears could you see? 1, 2, or all 4?

"Rhyme Time"

What if Woodrow were to decide to leave the ranch and look for a new job? Make a rhyme using "Woodrow" that would relate to his new job possibilities.

Example: Woodrow works in a salon doing pedicures.
Answer: Woodrow **TOE.**

1. Woodrow sells loaves of bread.

2. Woodrow runs a whitewater kayak business.

3. Woodrow sells a weed eliminating tool.

4. Woodrow sells plant fertilizer.

5. Woodrow makes decorative birthday candles.

6. Woodrow stars in a Broadway theatre.

7. Woodrow retrieves roadside broken-down cars.

Answers:

1. Woodrow DOUGH   2. Woodrow ROW   3. Woodrow HOE   4. Woodrow GROW   5. Woodrow BLOW   6. Woodrow SHOW   7. Woodrow TOW

Have you visited Hank's official website yet?

www.hankthecowdog.com

Don't miss out on exciting *Hank the Cowdog* games and activities, as well as up-to-date news about upcoming books in the series!

When you visit, you'll find:

- Hank's BLOG, which is the first place we announce upcoming books and new products!
- Hank's Official Shop, with tons of great *Hank the Cowdog* books, audiobooks, games, t-shirts, stuffed animals, mugs, bags, and more!
- Links to Hank's social media, whereby Hank sends out his "Cowdog Wisdom" to fans.
- A FREE, printable "Map of Hank's Ranch"!
- Hank's Music Page where you can listen to songs and even download FREE ringtones!
- A way to sign up for Hank's free email updates
- Sally May's "Ranch Roundup Recipes"!
- Printable & Colorable Greeting Cards for Holidays.

- Articles about Hank and author John R. Erickson in the news,

...AND MUCH, MUCH MORE!

BOOKS
The Collection

FAN ZONE
Fun & Games

AUTHOR
Meet the Creator

STORE
Books & More

search the website   GO

Find Toys, Games, Books & More
at the Hank shop.

ANNOUNCING: A sneak peek at Hank #66

Ever thought of having a Hank the Cowdog themed Party?

Hank Plays Cupid:

GAMES
COME PLAY WITH HANK & PALS

BOOKS
BROWSE THE ENTIRE HANK CATALOG

FRIENDS
GET TO KNOW THE RANCH GANG

FROM THE BLOG

JAN 26 Hank is Cupid in Disguise...

JAN 18 The Valentine's Day Robbery! - a Snippet from the Story

DEC 04 Getting SIGNED Hank the Cowdog books for Christmas!

OCT 14 Education Association's lists of recommended books?

VISIT THE BLOG

Hank's Survey
We'd love to know what you think!   GO

TEACHER'S CORNER

Download fun activity guides, discussion questions and more.

SALLY MAY'S RECIPES

Discover delicious recipes from Sally May herself.   GO

Hank's Music. ♪
Free ringtones, music and more!
MORE

Official Shop
Find books, audio, toys and more!
LET'S GO

Join Hank's Security Force
Get the activity letter and other cool stuff.
JOIN   SECURITY FORCE

 Visit Hank's Facebook page

 Follow Hank on Twitter

 Watch Hank on YouTube

 Follow Hank on Pinterest

 Send Hank an Email

Get the Latest

Keep up with Hank's news and promotions by signing up for our e-news.

Looking for The Hank Time fan club newsletter?

Enter your email address   SIGN UP

Hank in the News

 Find out what the media is saying about Hank.   GO

FEATURED BOOK

The Christmas Turkey Disaster

Now Available!

Hank is in real trouble this time. L...

BUY   READ   LISTEN

HANK

BOOKS
Browse Titles
Buy Books
Audio Samples

FAN ZONE
Games
Hank & Friends
Security Force

AUTHOR
John Erickson's Bio
Hank in the News
In Concert

SHOP
The Books
Store
Get Help

John R. Erickson,

a former cowboy, has written numerous books for both children and adults and is best known for his acclaimed *Hank the Cowdog* series. The *Hank* series began as a self-publishing venture in Erickson's garage in 1982 and has endured to become one of the nation's most popular series for children and families.

Through the eyes of Hank the Cowdog, a smelly, smart-aleck Head of Ranch Security, Erickson gives readers a glimpse into daily life on a cattle ranch in the West Texas Panhandle. His stories have won a number of awards, including the Audie, Oppenheimer, Wrangler, and Lamplighter Awards, and have been translated into Spanish, Danish, Farsi, and Chinese. In 2019, Erickson was inducted into the Texas Literary Hall of Fame. *USA Today* calls the *Hank the Cowdog* books "the best family entertainment in years." Erickson lives and works on his ranch in Perryton, Texas, with his family.

Nicolette G. Earley

was born and raised in the Texas Hill Country. She began working for Maverick Books in 2008, editing, designing new Hank the Cowdog books, and working with the artist who had put faces on all the characters: Gerald Holmes. When Holmes died in 2019, she discovered that she could reproduce his drawing style and auditioned for the job. She made

her debut appearance in Book 75, illustrating new books in the series she read as a child. She and her husband, Keith, now live in coastal Mississippi.